# 3 X 3

## THE PORCH SWING MYSTERIES
### BOOK THREE

## PATRICK E. CRAIG

# COPYRIGHT

# CONTENTS

# PRAISE FOR THE PORCH SWING MYSTERIES

*3 X 3*

The title of this book, *3 X 3*, intrigued me from the beginning, because I thought it was a mistake. But it is an integral part of the plot, and makes sense as the reader gets further into the book. The twists and turns of discovery kept me turning pages long into the night to find out all the answers. The Amish "Miss Marple", Jenny Hershberger, does her magic and figures out the mystery of "who dunnit" with straightforward no nonsense thinking. The writing is clear and direct, without a lot of extraneous fluff to make up a word count. I enjoyed this book and look forward to more of Craig's work.

— TENNEY COULON SINGER

Have you ever been on the edge of your seat as you watch a spellbinding movie? Well, the new book by Patrick E. Craig, *3 X 3*, gives you that same sense of foreboding. This story is so well crafted you forget you are reading a book. No, you are actually sitting in that movie theater holding your popcorn just waiting for the bucket to fly out of your hand as the screams fill the room.

— CHERESE AKHAVEIN

## THE BOY IN BLUE DENIM

Craig is able to skillfully combine the twists and turns of an Agatha Christie-Miss Marple murder mystery, and its suspense and edginess, with the rustic beauty of the Amish world and the aura of romance and peace that rests like a summer dew on its farms and homesteads. A page-turner not to be missed by fans of Amish fiction or fans of well-written murder mysteries both. A splendid effort by a seasoned author who excels at every genre he puts his hand to.

— MURRAY PURA CIBA, WORD GUILD,
SELAH AWARD-WINNING AUTHOR

**You could call it Amish fiction on steroids!** The Boy in Blue Denim is a page-turner for sure. I have always liked the author's style and thoroughness of research, but this time he brought it to a new level. His characters are engaging and interesting. Their lives are intertwined in ways you would not expect. I read the book in two sittings because each page demanded I find out more. There are twists and turns you will not be expecting, and I suspect you won't want to put it down either!

— CONNIE PORTER

## THE QUILT THAT KNEW

Patrick E. Craig has once again written a book that will take you deep into the heart of Amish country. *The Quilt That Knew* is a delightful and intriguing plain and simple mystery.

BUTCHER'S BRIDE, THE LEPER KING AND
LOVE ABIDETH STILL

# DEDICATION

Dedicated to my wife, Judy, who once again has labored alongside me to make this book the best it can be.

# ACKNOWLEDGEMENT

I would like to take the opportunity here to acknowledge a few of the men and women who have been intrumental in my development as an author.

First, to those who have passed: Zane Grey, Louis L'Amour, Harper Lee, Ken Kesey, Mark Twain, J.R.R. Tolkein, C.S. Lewis, Agatha Christie, William Shakespeare.

Then to those present: Murray Pura, Vannetta Chapman, Nick Harrison, James Scott Bell, Tim Riter, Jerry Jenkins.

# A NOTE FROM PATRICK E. CRAIG

Over the course of two Porch Swing Mysteries, Jenny Hershberger has established herself as the Amish Miss Marple.

In the first book Jenny solved the mystery of **The Quilt That Knew**, the case of a missing girl found buried in a box in the woods forty years after her disappearance. Then she solved the perplexing case of a little lost boy who was murdered in book two, **The Boy In Blue Denim.**

Now she is back in book three, *3 X 3,* and is facing the most dangerous killer she has so far encountered.

Jenny Hershberger has moved to Apple Creek, the small Amish Village in Wayne County, Ohio, where she spent her childhood, She has purchased her family home and hopes to find peace there.

But then a horrific new mystery comes her way. Three random killings, all marked by the bloody signature of a ruthless serial killer, electrify the little town of Wooster, Ohio. Elbert Wainwright, Jenny's counterpart on the Wooster police force, puts his team to work and quickly hunts down the man they think is responsible—a mentally disabled Vietnam War vet. All the evidence points to Steven Lambright.

But when Elbert calls Jenny and her old friend, retired sheriff Bobby Halverson, to help, the case against Lambright starts to go south as Jenny discovers there is much more to the story than meets the eye. One by one, Jenny uncovers secrets hidden for forty years, secrets deeply connected to the Amish community. And as she brings them to light, Jenny finds the past can reveal much about the present—in terrifying ways.

Patrick E. Craig

## NUMBER ONE

*A*n exceedingly dull day. Way too hot.

Detective Gary Linden sat in his office at the Wooster police station. Outside through the half-open Venetian blinds, a glaring sun shone feebly through the dusty mid-Ohio harvest haze. The 92 degree temperature paralyzing Wooster was wholly out of character for a late August day and Gary could hear the ancient AC in the attic above laboring to keep up. The occasional sweat drop running down into his once-pressed collar let him know the machine was not doing its job. The phone rang.

"Detective Linden."

"Hey, Gary, John Ashe."

"John! What's up?"

"It's 4:52 p.m. on an unusually hot Thursday in Wooster and I thought you might be up for a couple of cold brewskis down at Muddy's when you close up over there."

Gary nodded his head. "That sounds like a glorious end to a very dull day. Let's meet around..."

The door cracked open and the office girl's head poked

through... then her hand—from which protruded several pieces of mail. "Elbert sent these over for you to look through, Detective... if you have time, of course."

"Sure. I always have time for Lieutenant Wainwright."

Gary counted the envelopes.

*Five. One minute per envelope, add ten minutes in case paperwork is involved... ten minutes to get out of here, ten minutes to Muddy's...*

"John?"

"Yeah, bro."

"How does 5:45 sound? Some last minutes just walked through the door."

"Okay, see you there. I'll start without you."

"Thanks, buddy."

Charlene gave him her trademark smirk as she handed him the stack. "You might be a little late, Detective."

"Uh, how long have you had these on your desk, Charlene?"

Charlene smiled demurely. "Why, since the mail came this morning."

"And you didn't bring them right up because...?"

A shrug, the pouty look. "Well, you know how Lieutenant Wainwright keeps me busy..."

Gary shook his head. *He gives you longer coffee breaks if you torment me...*

He began sorting through the stack, checking the return addresses.

*The Mahoning Valley Scrappers—probably looking for some off-duty cops to do security.*

He zipped it open with his letter opener and scanned it.

*Yep. I'll put this one up on the bulletin board.*

The second letter was junk mail.

The third letter, addressed in all capital, hand-printed

letters, read, "TO THE SMARTEST COP IN WOOSTER—IF THERE IS ONE!"

He set it aside and looked at the other two pieces. Another mailer, this one from a window coverings company, and an invitation to test some new hearing aids for a free dinner. Trash can. Then Gary picked up the hand-addressed envelope and opened it. Inside was a single eight-and-a-half inch by eleven-inch sheet, folded three times. Gary unfolded it. There was a brief laser-printed note.

*I am going to kill three women. The first will be soon. Springs is here. 3 X 3*

Gary read it again.

*Who would send us this stuff? And he misspelled Spring.*

Gary read the letter one more time, re-folded it, and put it back in the envelope.

*Boy, some people need to get out more often.*

He took out the request for off-duty cops at the baseball stadium, gathered up the remaining mail, leaned over the corner of his desk and dropped them all in the trash. Then he got up, walked out into the hall to the bulletin board, pinned up the note from the Scrappers, and went back into his office. He put his things away, put his department-issued Glock in the drawer, and went to the door. His hand went to the light switch, but he paused. Something...

Gary went back to the trash can and fished out the murder threat envelope, looked at the scrawled address one more time and then put it in the bottom side drawer of his desk.

*I better hang on to it in case Elbert asks me about it.*

Then he left.

Gary's buddy, John, was two beers down the road when Gary got to Muddy's. They moved from the bar to a booth. The waitress ambled over and took his order.

"Corona Extra with a lime slice and could you put it in the freezer for five minutes before you bring it?"

John grinned. "When you want an ice cold beer, you mean it."

In five minutes, the beer came. It was cold enough that the beer half-froze around the lime slice.

*A cold one!*

Gary sat, enjoying it.

John pulled out a pack of Camels and offered one to Gary, who declined. "So, what's new at Wooster Central, Gary, ol' pal?"

"Not much. Lieutenant Wainwright has something against me, I think. Anyway, he keeps sending the office tart into my space with all kinds of 'extra' stuff to do, at the last minute, of course. Answer mail, call the help center to see how they are doing, review the work tapes of the 911 operators—real high-end stuff. And every bit has zero meaning attached."

"But, nothing skanky or weird?"

"Well... I got a strange letter today. They addressed it to the smartest cop in Wooster."

John laughed. "Well, at least they gave it to you. What was in it?"

"Typical off-the-wall letter stuff. 'I'm going to murder three women, and the first one will be soon.' The odd thing was it also said 'Springs is here.'"

John shook his head. "Just some nut-ball. Can't even get the seasons straight."

THE WHITE VAN PULLED INTO A PARKING SPACE ON THE ROAD TO the park. The driver turned off the motor and waited.

The young woman parked her bike at the entrance to Grosjean Park. She carefully put the steel cable bike lock through one of the bicycle stands provided for hikers and then through the front wheel of her bike. She took the small backpack from the back of the bike and slipped her bare arms through the loops. White shorts, a blue short-sleeved button-up blouse and hiking boots. She wore a blue baseball cap with her ponytail pulled through between the cap and the size-adjusting strap. Pretty, athletic looking, she checked the bike lock one more time and then headed up the trail for Johnson Springs.

The driver of the van waited for a few minutes and then got out. Tall, dressed for summer, with a broad-brimmed safari hat pulled low over his eyes and hiding his face, he walked up the same path the girl had taken and disappeared into the woods.

The girl walked about fifteen minutes until she came to the sign pointing to Johnson Springs. It was an enchanted spot where two or three year-round springs bubbled up through the limestone formations so prevalent in the park. Clear and pure, they ran together and then dropped over a short limestone ledge into a deep pool before twisting their way down the hill and emptying into Apple Creek. This was her special place, and she came here often. She took off her pack and her shoes and then sat at the edge of the pool with her feet in the water. It was delicious. Cold.

She didn't hear the footsteps until the person was right behind her. She turned, looking straight into the afternoon sun. She could barely see the face because of the afternoon light behind it, but she recognized it. A little tinge of fear, but she spoke.

"Hello. Nice day, isn't it? I've seen you before, haven't I? Down in the parking lot..."

There was the sound of feet rustling the fallen leaves, then a gasp and feet splashing in the water... kicking, a muffled shriek...

Then silence.

---

Saturday morning in Wooster, still hot. Detective Linden did not like the fact that his phone was ringing at 7:30 in the morning of his day off. He let it go to the answering machine.

"Linden! This is Lieutenant Wainwright. I need you down at Grosvenor Park. We have a murder on our hands. At Johnson Springs."

Detective Gary Linden sat bolt upright in his bed and grabbed the phone before the Lieutenant could hang up.

"This is Linden, Lieutenant Wainwright. Sorry, I was occupied."

"Did you hear my message?"

"Yes, a murder? At Johnson springs?"

"That's right. I'm heading over now. Meet you there."

"I have to stop by the office. There's something I have to show you."

"Okay, but make it quick."

---

Gary found two police cars with lights flashing, an ambulance, and Lieutenant Wainwright's Suburban parked in the lot at the trailhead. A uniformed officer waited at the head of the trail. He pointed.

"The Lieutenant is about a hundred yards up the trail."

Gary took to the path and walked the short distance to the scene. Crime tape surrounded the clearing that faced the Springs and Lieutenant Wainwright huddled with Dr. Wilkins, the department's forensic pathologist. They were kneeling by a body. Elbert stood up as Gary approached.

"Detective Linden, nice you could come."

*He has never liked me.*

"Sorry it took so long, Lieutenant, but I stopped by the office to get something you need to see."

Elbert extended his hand. "Well?"

Gary handed over the envelope. Elbert looked at the hand-printed address and then took out the letter and read it. He read it again and then looked up at Gary.

"This didn't excite your interest when it came?"

"I thought it was a nut-job. I see dozens of letters like this every year."

"Why didn't you toss it then?"

Gary hesitated. "I... I don't know, just a feeling."

Elbert smiled. "That, my dear detective, is called 'coply' instinct. Glad to see it's functioning. I assume you thought he misspelled Spring?"

"Well, yes. How would I know he really meant Johnson Springs?"

"You are assuming it's a he?"

Gary looked down at the body. The girl's shorts were still in place, but her blouse was partly unbuttoned. Her hands were bound behind her with gray duct tape and her ankles tied together with what looked like orange and black poly-ester rope. A piece of the same tape was over her mouth. The rope looped tightly around her neck and drew her ankles up almost to her waist behind her. There were bloodstains on the blouse. No bra underneath.

"Hog-tied, helpless. She looks athletic, in-shape. It would take somebody big, strong to overpower her. A man."

Elbert nodded. "Interesting."

"Has she been... you know... molested?"

Elbert shook his head. "The doc says no. She died of strangulation. And the mud at the bottom of the pond by the bank was all stirred up. She must have been sitting with her feet in the water when the killer came up from behind. She struggled, but the killer got the rope over her neck and she was unconscious in just a few seconds."

"Why all the extra tape and rope, if he killed her right off?"

Elbert shook his head. "Got me."

"Got a name?"

Elbert pulled out a small notebook. "Anna Myerson. Age twenty, lives in Wooster, attends Wooster College. I need you to do a complete canvas. Family, friends, classmates. We need to find out if someone wanted to kill her or if this is just random."

Gary shook his head. "I don't think it's random because he mentioned the springs in his note. I'll find out if she's come here before. If she has, the killer may have been tracking her."

Elbert looked down at the dead girl. "Okay, good." He looked at the note again. "The killer says he's going to kill three women. And we know this is from the killer."

Gary was puzzled. "How do we know?"

Elbert pointed to the signature. Then he spoke to the doctor. "Show him, Doc."

"I've got all the pictures I need, Lieutenant. Can I untie her?"

Elbert nodded. Dr. Wilkins undid the rope around her neck and released her bent legs. Then he unwrapped the tape from her wrists and put it into an evidence bag. Finally, he straightened the girl out and gently rolled her onto her back. The bloodstains on her blouse were more evident. Dr. Wilkins pulled her blouse back. On her chest above her left breast, it looked like she was badly scratched, but blood obscured the scratches. Dr. Wilkins carefully wiped it away until Gary could see what the marks were. The killer had marked something onto the girl's skin with the point of something very sharp, just below her collarbone.

3 X 3.

## APPLE CREEK DREAMS

*J*enny Hershberger sighed, spread the letter out on the table, and read it again. It was from her cousin Jared in Apple Creek, Ohio. She stared at it for a long time. The letter was brief and to the point, as were all of Jared's communications. But it was also lovely and kind.

*Dear Jenny,*

*Evangeline and I have been talking about the old house, your folks' place. My Uncle Levi bought the place from you when you moved to Pennsylvania. He hoped to keep the whole Hershberger farm as one property. When we were first married, Evangeline and I lived in the small house Uncle Reuben built and we loved being there. Then, when Uncle Levi died, he left the property to us. We moved up to the big house and left your old place empty. We have tried to keep it as your mama Jerusha did, but now, with all our children and the increased responsibilities of the farm, the upkeep has become hard for us. So, we have separated it from the entire piece of land and will soon put it on the market as a separate property. We don't want to sell it, but circumstances dictate we do. So, that said, we are offering it to you first and we will sell it to you at appraised, not market value. We would love for you to have it.*

*Jared.*

It was simple. Jared was offering her the old Springer home in Apple Creek, the house and property where she grew up. And the price was very generous. Jenny's heart beat fast.

*My old house... in Apple Creek. Oh, my.*

She stared at the letter for a long time, her heart beating rapidly and her emotions swirling.

So many memories in that house. Her papa had built it with his own hands. Every board and every nail was dedicated to Reuben's love for her mama, Jerusha. And then when the Springers adopted her, it became the center of her life. She loved the farm in Paradise that her grandfather Borntraeger had left for her and Jonathan. But her heart was truly in Apple Creek.

There was a knock on the door that brought Jenny back from her reverie. Jenny sighed. She really wasn't in the mood for company, but she went to the door and opened it. Standing on the porch was her daughter, Rachel. She was carrying a pan covered with a towel.

"Rachel?"

"Hi, Mama. I hope I'm not intruding... I was in the area with Levon and I felt like I should come see you. So, I had him drop me off."

Jenny opened the screen and grabbed her daughter's arm. "Oh, Rachel! You don't know how much I needed to see you today." She pulled Rachel through the door, almost dragging her surprised daughter into the house.

"*Kumme,* I need to show you something."

She pushed her daughter into the kitchen and pulled out a chair. Then she placed Jared's letter in front of her.

"Tell me what you think."

Rachel scanned the letter and then looked up at Jenny, her mouth open. "Mama! They want to sell you your old house!"

Jenny nodded. "I was just reading it and to tell you the truth, *es hat mich völlig durcheinander gebracht.*"

Rachel nodded her head up and down. "It would fluster me too, Mama. What are you going to do?"

"I don't know, Rachel. I'm torn, so torn."

"I can see why, Mama."

Jenny looked at her lovely daughter. Rachel was in her mid-forties now, but still as youthful as a child. The years had been kind, even with three children.

"I lived there too, and I also love that house..." Rachel paused. "But Mama, if you buy it, you will move to Ohio? What about Bobby? And us?"

"I know, Rachel, I know. So many things to consider. I love this place too. Your papa and I shared all our life together here. And here in Paradise are my daughter, my Daniel, my grandchildren, and Uncle Bobby." Jenny smiled. "Maybe a cup of *kaffee* would calm me down. And whatever you have in that pan that smells so good..."

Rachel pulled the towel back. "*Kaffee kuchen.* I made it this morning."

"Did I hear someone say coffee cake?"

The two women turned. Bobby Halverson was standing in the kitchen doorway. At eighty-three, Bobby still had a military bearing and a commanding presence. Her father's best friend since their days in the Marine Corps, and almost a father to her, Bobby had lived in the cottage on Jenny's farm since her husband Jonathan had died, fifteen years before.

Jenny got up. "This must be an important decision. Everybody that is concerned is being drawn here by it."

Bobby looked puzzled. "What decision? I was just walking by and smelled the cake."

Jenny pulled out a chair. "Sit down, Uncle Bobby, and read this while I get us some *kaffee*. Rachel, you better cut us some of that cake. You know where the plates are."

Jenny pushed the letter in front of Bobby and then went to the cupboard for mugs. Bobby skimmed the letter and then re-read it. He looked up. "The old house, eh? Well, this is an interesting offer. What are you going to do?"

"I told Rachel that I'm going in a lot of different directions. I love the Paradise farm, I have many memories with Jonathan and my daughter and grandchildren here. I've made a life for myself and I've been content. But two things are tearing at me."

Bobby took the cup Jenny offered and then smiled. "Numero uno, Jared has to sell the house, and that means it will be gone forever unless you buy it."

Jenny shook her head. "Uncle Bobby, how do you know me so well?"

"I was the third one in Apple Creek you met when you were only four years old. I've watched you become a brilliant researcher and writer. I've rescued you from gangsters. I helped you find your birth mother, and I was there when you found Jonathan, missing for eight years. I guess that nothing in your life has ever escaped me. I know how you think."

"Oh yes? Well, what's the second thing?"

"Jonathan's buried here, but your folks are buried there."

Rachel laughed. "Uncle Bobby is like your conscience. If you move, you better take him with you."

"Yes, well, he didn't get the second thing right."

"Oh, really?" said Bobby.

"No, you didn't. What you said is the third thing. My second thing is, what will I do if you don't come with me?"

"Me?"

"Uncle Bobby, if I move back to Apple Creek, you have to come with me. There's a house out back we can fix up for you and the elders of Apple Creek will be a lot more understanding of an *Englischer* sharing my property than they are here. Oh, yes, they put up with you, but only because you live way up the hill. But I've seen them looking at you when you aren't looking."

Bobby smiled. "Well, I've felt them looking at me when I wasn't looking."

They all laughed.

"If I buy the place, I will only buy it if you come with me, so please say you will if I do."

"Okay, I'll consider it." He looked at Rachel, who was nodding her head vigorously up and down. "I guess Rachel wants me to go."

"Mama needs you, Uncle Bobby. And I wouldn't worry about her being alone if she had you."

Jenny sat at the table. "Okay, all the cards are on the table. Now I need to broach the subject with *du leiber Gott* and see what He tells me."

"I think he already knows," said Bobby, "and I think you do too."

THAT NIGHT IN BED, JENNY COULD NOT SLEEP. SHE WAS thinking of Apple Creek. She remembered that all her childhood was imbued with a sense of being settled and permanent, that somehow that permanence escaped her in Paradise.

All the bright days of her youth sat in the mystery of God's eternal circle of life and death, winter and spring, summer and fall. She remembered the cycles of the seasons and how they dictated the deepest feelings in her heart, with her days marked not by events, but by smells and colors and sounds and all the other sensory signals.

The temperature of a morning's rising told her everything about the day ahead, be it the coolness of a daybreak in spring; the heat of the long, languid days of summer; the crisp bite of a fall day; or the chill of winter that pushed her with icy fingers back under the welcoming warmth of her lovely down quilt—a quilt made by the loving hands of her mother, Jerusha.

She remembered propping herself on the window sill and listening to the lilting chirp of a robin outside her open bedroom window or the haunting call of the Canadian geese heading south, sounds that manifested the procession of days to Jenny more surely than any calendar.

The solemn silence of a winter night, with her shoes softly crunching on the snow as she made her way toward the light in the window ahead, or the grinding of the machinery and the smell of the thick harvest dust, the dust that covered her papa's face and arms before he washed up after a day in the fields... these things marked the passage of time and bound Jenny surely to the beloved land of Apple Creek and the life so graciously granted by the Master of the vineyard.

She lay awake and thought of the beauty of Apple Creek

in the fall. The leaves of the Buckeye trees turning bright red, and the green, spiked pods that hid the green spikey horse chestnuts splitting open and dropping their beautiful seeds on the ground. Being a child again, raking the leaves into forts and piling up the shiny brown nuts to barter with friends from down the street.

Fall mornings always came armed with the warning bite of winter yet to come, the air filled with the promise of families gathered at festive tables and the wonder of frosty nights that delight Jenny's heart with cathedrals of starry splendor. And end of fall would bring the soft snow to blanket all living things in the quiet death of winter; but for Jenny, fall had been the summation of life in Apple Creek, for fall was harvest time, when the cycle of life was at its peak. Gathering in the harvest, working with her mama to put up corn and meat and fruit for the winter. Laughing with joy and feeling the strength and warmth of her papa's arms as he embraced his girls after a hard day in the fields.

Jared's letter had arrived just in time for fall and Jenny knew that soon the fields surrounding Apple Creek would ripen with bounty—the air heavy with the fecundity of the yearly progression coming to its fullness.

Somehow, to Jenny, it was as though her memories of Apple Creek captured the lovely village in a backwater eddy of time and now that village slowly drifted in a lovely continuity of days while the main current of civilization rushed by into an unknown future.

Here papa and mama were part of the land, she was linked to the land, and the land was forever. The fields of Apple Creek stretched to the horizon, and the days were like the fields, reaching back into the permanence of the past and extending forward into a future that she knew held the same tasks, the same demands, the same feasts, and the same succession of birth, life, and death.

A picture came to Jenny: she was sitting with Reuben and Jerusha in the hospital on the day they passed. She remembered this—her parents were not afraid of death, for they had their God and His promises, they had the land and its harvest each year, and they had their daughter, and they were content. And above everything, they had the simplicity of their way. And it was enough.

Jenny sat up in her bed. The sense of Apple Creek pervaded her room, like the smell of lilacs wafting in a window on an April morning.

*Home! I need to go home.*

# NUMBER TWO

There was a buzz on Detective Gary Linden's intercom.

*What does Wainwright want now?*

Linden pushed down the button. "Linden."

"Hey, Detective, I have something here you need to see."

"Be right down, Lieutenant."

Gary got up, checked his tie in the mirror by the door of his office, and walked out into the hall. The unusual August heat wave had continued unabated and there were a lot of open office doors in the hallway, a tribute to the failed A/C. Conversations leaked from them and melded into a general hum in the building.

Down the stairs, turn right, big office—almost a corner. 'Lieutenant Elbert Wainwright' on the door. Charlene, the watchdog, sat at her desk outside the office, looking like a pouty Windsor Palace guard. Gary remembered her penchant for bringing him his mail at 4:59 pm.

"Any late mail for me, Charlene?"

She scowled and pointed at the door. "In there, he's waiting."

*Bad day at Black Rock, eh?*

He knocked.

"Come."

Lieutenant Elbert Wainwright sat behind his desk. He didn't really have any attitudes, because he had been a detective a long time before his promotion. The two big cases he had solved, the girl in the box, and the boy in blue denim, had put his name up in lights to the powers-that-be and now he was a lieutenant. No, not really any attitudes, but it seemed like he just didn't like Gary.

"Lieutenant?"

"Sit down, Detective." Gary slipped into the chair in front of the desk. It was set low, so Elbert had the advantage of looking down. The Lieutenant slid an envelope across the desk. Gary recognized the handwriting.

"3 X 3?"

"Yep. And he's telling us he's going to do it again."

Gary looked at the handwritten address, all caps.

DETECTIVE GARY LINDEN—OBVIOUSLY NOT THE SMARTEST COP IN WOOSTER.

"It's addressed to you, but Charlene brought it in when she recognized the handwriting. I opened it. Tell me what you think."

The message was a note and a doggerel... from an old nursery rhyme.

*Dear Gary, I just can't help myself. I've got to do it again.*

*One TWO, Buckle My Shoes. 3 X 3*

Elbert tapped a pencil on his desk impatiently. "Well, what do you make of it?"

Gary looked up. "He said he was going to kill three

women. This is obviously a reference to number two. He put in a misquoted nursery rhyme. Not very helpful."

Elbert shook his head. "Gary, do you ever get the impression that I don't like you?"

Gary felt the heat in his face. He knew he had just flushed red. "Well, now that you mention it…"

"It's not that I don't like you…" Elbert sighed. "It's just that I get impatient with you. You have the makings of an excellent police officer, but…"

Gary grimaced. "Go on…"

"You don't think things through. When you got that first letter, you threw it in the trash, didn't you?"

"Yes, but I…"

"Yes, you dug it back out, probably just before you walked out the door and headed for the bar. Actually, that was the first time since you've been on staff here that I saw an actual police instinct kick in. It gave me hope."

"Well, I'm glad I did something right."

Elbert smiled, and it put Gary at ease… a bit. "Look, Gary, I was a detective for a long time, much longer than most policemen are. I'm forty-nine years old. The average age of a police lieutenant is forty-five. I was a uniform for ten years and a detective for fifteen. I didn't like it, but in the long run it helped me. I got to be on the street longer and I got to tackle some cases that gave me an actual head's up on how to think like a policeman should."

"Yeah, the girl in the box and the boy in blue denim."

"That's right, and do you know how I solved them?"

"Well, I heard you had some help."

Elbert laughed. "Help? Man, I got to work with a little Amish woman who has the sharpest intuitive sense that I have ever seen—a mind like a steel trap and a willingness to dig as deep as it takes to get to the bottom of things. And she brought with her an eighty-two-year-old ex-sheriff, ex-marine who won the Silver Star on Guadalcanal. Tough as they come and with coply instincts that blew my mind. Between the two of them, I was in awe. I never would have solved anything without them. Bobby Halverson showed me how to think like a cop, and Jenny Hershberger taught me how to see the next step, how to follow up clues that most people would miss, and how to ask for things that nobody ever asks for—like in Danny Wittmer's case."

"The boy in blue denim?"

"Right. We figured out that he was Danny Wittmer, buried in a grave in Indiana for ten years, and murdered by a psycho killer who had assumed the identity of Danny's real father. That was as far as we took it. When we disinterred Danny to bury him with his parents, it was Jenny who insisted that we do a DNA sample. Something just told her."

Gary nodded. "And you found out that it wasn't Danny, right?"

"Exactly. If we hadn't taken that one last step, Danny Wittmer would have lived out his life in the Apple Creek Center, not thirty minutes from here, never being reunited with his family and sitting in a chair totally withdrawn from the world. And we never would have known who the boy in blue denim really was. That's what I'm talking about—going the extra mile."

Gary looked down. "So I don't do that?"

Elbert shook his head. "Not yet. That's what I'm trying to get across here. Take, for instance, this second letter. Your take is he's threatening to kill another woman, and he added a misquoted nursery rhyme. But don't you remember what he misspelled in the first letter, what he added?"

Gary thought. "Oh yeah, Springs is coming..." He

thought for a minute. "It was a clue, wasn't it? The girl was murdered at Johnson Springs."

"That's right, and you thought he was a moron who couldn't spell. So what did he say in this one?"

"One Two Buckle my shoes..." Gary had a thought. "Another clue? Something about shoes or buckles or..."

"Do you know why someone wrote that nursery rhyme?"

"No."

"To help kids learn to count. One, two, buckle my shoe, three, four, open the door..."

The penny dropped for Gary. "So something about schools or teaching or..."

"Keep going, Gary. Kids learn to count in..."

"Well, it would have to be in preschool because when they come to first grade, they should already know how. So... 3 X 3 is going to kill a preschool teacher?"

"Bingo. So what do you have to do?"

"I have to find the names of all the preschools in the area and see if there is a tie-in?"

"Is that a question, Gary, or a revelation?"

"Revelation, Lieutenant."

"Right answer, Detective." Elbert looked at his wristwatch. "It's 11:00. I'd say you got some research to do before the end of the day. And I want your report on my desk before you go."

"You got it." Gary stood up. Elbert had gone back to some paperwork. He started for the door.

"Gary?"

He turned.

"I hope our conversation has given you some insights today. I'll be looking for it in your future work."

"Yes, Lieutenant."

Elbert chuckled. "And just to show you my heart's in the

right place, I won't have Charlene bring you late mail anymore."

"I'd appreciate that, Lieutenant."

"You know, Gary... I almost wish this crime had something to do with the Amish. I'd love to have you follow Jenny and Bobby around for a couple of weeks."

———

Liz Ingersoll finished packing up the toys lying around the room. She frowned as the odor of sour milk drifted up from the rug. She called out to Carol Watson, who was dusting off the chalkboard in the other room.

"I'll have to use the carpet cleaner on this place where Jimmy spilled his milk. It already stinks."

Carol called back. "Can you do it without me? I have to take my son to a soccer match."

"Sure, no problem. It won't take me long. Go ahead, I'll lock up when I leave."

"Thanks, Liz. You're a doll. I'll make it up, I promise."

Liz Ingersoll had only been working at Buckle My Shoe Preschool for three months. She had grown up in Wooster, but lived away for many years. Now she was home. A woman in her fifties, she had loved coming to work at the school and being around children again. It reminded her of her childhood, growing up in a close community with lots of children around...

*But all that's gone a long time ago.*

She went to the closet and got out the carpet cleaner the school used for just such events—spilled milk, the occasional sick child, or the little one that didn't get to the potty on time. She checked to make sure the water chamber was full. Then she added the cleaning solution. Before she started, she heard Carol shout goodbye as the door slammed behind her. Then she started up the machine and cleaned the still damp spot. The machine hummed quietly as Liz worked. She finished the area she was working on, turned off the machine, and unplugged it. She wrapped the cord around the cord holders and carried the cleaner to the closet, put it in, and closed the door. Liz heard a sound behind her and turned. Someone was standing behind her. Her heart leaped. Then she saw who it was. That face! She felt her heart race.

"You! What in the world are you doing here...?"

"I told you I would find you. I told you that you would never get away from me."

"But you... you're dead... dead!!"

The figure stepped in close... reached out. "Back from the grave, Lizzie. I promised I would kill you. I always keep my promises."

"Don't... please..."

Those were Liz Ingersoll's last words.

***

GARY HAD TAKEN HEART AT THE LIEUTENANT'S TALK. HE FELT better about his career and he felt inspired to do some proper police work. So he spent the afternoon digging up all the preschools in Wayne County. At one point, he felt a tinge of excitement when he came across a preschool franchise called Buckle My Shoe Preschool.

*This has to be it!*

He checked on the website and found that there were two of them in the Wooster area.

*Buckle my shoes, not shoe. So, two to choose from.*

He wrote the info on a sheet of paper and then called Elbert. "I think I found something I'd like to show you."

"Come on down."

In a few minutes, Gary was in Elbert's office, showing him what he found.

"We need to contact both those schools at once. You call the one on Chase Street and I will get the one on Williams..."

Just then, the intercom buzzed.

"Yes, Charlene?"

"There's a call for you, Lieutenant, a woman. She sounds hysterical."

Elbert picked up the phone.

"Lieutenant Wainwright... Hold on ma'am, you'll have to slow down... You found who?... Liz Ingersoll... She's dead, murdered? Where are you calling from? Okay, we'll be right over."

Elbert put down the phone. "We're too late. They found a woman murdered at the Buckle My Shoe Preschool on Chase Street. Let's go."

---

GARY LOOKED DOWN AT LIZ INGERSOLL'S BODY. SAME M.O. Her hands were bound behind her with gray duct tape and her ankles tied together with orange and black polyester rope. Again, there was a piece of the tape over her mouth. The rope looped tightly around her neck and drew her ankles and feet up almost to her waist behind her. Her skirt was still on, but the woman's white blouse was unbuttoned and her bra exposed. There were bloodstains.

"Carol Watson, the woman who found her, works here as a teacher. She had to leave early to take her son to a soccer game. When she left, Liz was cleaning the carpet. When she got to the game, she discovered she had left her purse, so she drove back to pick it up. She says she couldn't have been gone more than forty-five minutes. When she came in, she found Liz Ingersoll like this."

Just then, Doctor Wilkins walked in. He bent to his task and, in a few minutes, confirmed the cause of death.

"She was strangled first and then hog-tied like Anna Myerson."

"Why does he do that after they are dead?" asked Gary.

The doctor frowned. "I don't know, some sort of signature or something?" The police photographer snapped several pictures and then the doctor untied her. He straightened the body out and rolled her over on her back. Doctor Wilkins opened the blouse and pulled it back. He wiped away the blood. There it was.

3 X 3.

4

# HOME AGAIN

Jenny walked around the house, touching things, looking in closets.

*You're mine again! I didn't know how much I missed you, old Springer House.*

She went into her parents' room. Thanks to Jared's and Evangeline's meticulous care, everything was as Jenny had left it. She looked around.

"I should put up some of my mama's things. I wonder if those boxes are still out in the shed?"

Just then, there was the creaking of the screen door in the kitchen. She went down the hall and found Bobby coming into the house.

"Well?"

Bobby nodded. "That place will suit me fine. Evangeline changed your dad's shop into a sewing cottage and added some comforts so she could spend as much time there as needed. They sheet-rocked and painted the walls. There's a kitchenette with a small propane stove and refrigerator, a serviceable bathroom, a sitting room with a wood-burning stove, a very comfortable easy chair, a big throw rug, and a small bedroom. Rufus can stretch out his old bones by the fire." Bobby grinned. "And me, too. Everything an old man needs. And ten steps across the backyard to an Amish kitchen. How good does it get?"

"So, it will work for you?"

Bobby nodded. "Yep."

Moving to Apple Creek happened swiftly once Jenny bought her folks' old house. She gave Jared the earnest money and sealed the deal. There was enough money left from Jonathan's success in the publishing business to pay cash. Then she set up her grandsons to run the Paradise farm. Levon, her oldest, moved into the house. And just before they were ready to move, Rachel came with some wonderful news.

"Daniel has gone into business with another Morgan horse breeder, Mama. And he's going to be the managing partner, so he will spend a lot of time working there. And guess where the man has his breeding farm?"

Jenny shook her head. "I can't guess, Rachel."

Rachel took her mother's hand. "Millersburg, Ohio!"

"But Rachel! That's only twenty minutes from Apple Creek by buggy!"

"I know, Mama, I know." Rachel was almost jumping up and down in her excitement. "We will have to be there at least four months every year. Daniel's brothers and the boys will run the King farm while we are gone."

"Oh Rachel! You and Daniel can come and stay with me. There's plenty of room."

"Oh, and one more thing."

"What?"

"Levon is courting Amanda Troyer. He finally got up the nerve to talk to her and found out she's been waiting for three years for him to show an interest. They will be married next fall, I'm thinking."

"Oh, Rachel, our boy raising his family in the Borntraeger house. *Gott is gut!*"

"*Ja*, Mama, *sehr gut.*"

Jenny marveled at how quickly things fell together. She worried about Bobby being too old to move again, but he very much liked the idea of coming back to Ohio where he was born and raised. "It's good for a man to come back to his roots, I think. Anyway, I want you to bury me by my folks in the Wooster graveyard. I bought my plot years ago. Moving here makes it easy. Now you won't have to have someone drive me over from Pennsylvania in a hearse."

And so it was settled. In late August, Jenny and Bobby drove up the driveway to the old house. The pink ladies were blooming in the bed by the side of the house. The leaves on the Buckeye tree in the front yard gained that first fall blush, and the spiky balls were splitting. Soon the horse chestnuts would cover the ground. Neighborhood kids were raking leaves into piles. It was just as Jenny remembered that night in Paradise, and her heart filled with wonder.

Jared mowed the grass and cleaned out the cracks between the flagstones leading from the driveway to the front porch before they arrived. The old porch swing, built by her papa, moved in the slight breeze as though someone were sitting there.

Inside, the house smelled fresh, and Jenny knew Evangeline had done a thorough cleaning to welcome her home. The only recent addition was a propane refrigerator. The old wood-burning stove still stood in its place and the woodbox was full of freshly split kindling. Outside in the back, the woodpile was ready for winter and tarped over.

"It's as though I never left."

Jenny went out to the storage shed behind her papa's old workshop to see if any of her mama's things were still there. Surprisingly, the boxes were where she left them, still neatly arranged on the shelves, just as she packed them thirty-five years before. The only change was the dust that covered them. She took down some boxes, looking for those labeled *Jerusha.*

*Here they are.*

She looked around. There were some rags lying on a shelf in the corner, so she got them and wiped the dust off three of the boxes. She knew what was in them, because she had packed them and listed the contents on the box. When she pulled the last one down, the light from the open door glinted off something hanging on the wall behind the shelves. She pushed the other boxes aside and looked closer. There it was, hanging on a nail that had been driven into the stud supporting the back wall. She reached in and brought it out. It was an old-fashioned looking key with a metal circle at the end of the shaft. It had a tag attached to it with string. She read the tag. It was Reuben's handwriting.

*Jenny. Rose lock.*

A key... It was for her, but her papa had never given it to her.

*We built these shelves to hold the boxes when I left, but they weren't here when Papa worked in here. He must have put this up on the nail and forgotten about it. I wonder what 'Rose lock' means.*

She slipped the key into her apron pocket and turned her attention back to Jerusha's boxes. She picked one up and carried it out of the shed and into the kitchen. Bobby looked up from a cup of coffee.

"Need any help?"

"Yes, I have a couple more boxes in the shed on the floor.

They have some of my mama's things and I want to put them in her room."

Bobby went out and returned carrying the boxes. He followed Jenny into Jerusha's room and set the boxes on the floor.

"Thanks, Uncle Bobby. I just thought it would be nice to see some of Mama's treasures again."

Jenny spent the next hour going through the boxes and bringing out some special items. In one box, she found a knitted shawl that Jerusha made for Jenny when she was ten. It was, like all of Jerusha's work, beautifully done.

*I forgot about this shawl. She made it for me to wear to church on freezing days.*

The shawl had squares knit together: light brown, dark green, dark brown, and three shades of pink. Jenny draped it around her shoulders and remembered her mama putting it on her for the first time.

*"IT'S BEAUTIFUL, MAMA. BUT EVERYTHING YOU MAKE IS beautiful."*

*Jerusha had taken Jenny in her arms. "Hush Tochter. We must not give glory where glory is not due. My grössmütter Hannah, once told me. 'You have been given a way to give back to the Lord, as He has given to you. This is a special gift not given to everyone. But to whom much is given, much is required. You must always give back to God from the gift He has given you. And there are dangers along the way. If you become a good quilter or excel at anything, it is quite possible for you to become prideful, thinking that somehow you are more special than others. That is why we put a slight mistake in our quilts before we finish. This is so we do not make God angry with us for being too proud.' I have always remembered that."*

*Jenny felt her mother's heart beating close to hers. "I will try to remember, Mama, though it is hard for me sometimes."*

Jenny sat on the edge of the bed with the shawl wrapped around her.

*Oh, Mama. It has been thirty years and I miss you every day. I wish I could feel your arms around me once more.*

A picture came into her mind, the hospital room where her mama and papa died together. Bobby was standing with her. She remembered the last time Jerusha spoke to her.

*Her mama's eyes opened, and she looked at Jenny and Bobby.*

*"Take care of my girl, Bobby. She will need you."*

*Jenny slipped to her knees by Jerusha's side. "Mama, please... don't go."*

*The sweet hand that had comforted Jenny as long as she could remember reached out and softly stroked Jenny's cheek.*

*"I won't say do not grieve, Jenny. I know you will. But I must go. Reuben is waiting for me, and Jenna, too. And we will wait for you. Always remember that I love you."*

*Jenny looked at Jerusha.*

*"Mama, please..."*

*Jerusha smiled at Jenny and then closed her eyes. Jenny could hear the monitor beeping, marking the beat of Jerusha's heart, and Jenny remembered how safe she felt in every storm when her mama held her close. Her mama's heart.*

*She heard the monitor beep once, twice, and then it stopped.*

*Jerusha was gone.*

*A nurse came rushing in, looked at the monitor and called the doctor. They gathered around Jerusha. Finally, Doctor Beck turned to Jenny and Bobby.*

*"I'm sorry, Mrs. Hershberger,"* he said, the words coming at her from a long way away and echoing strangely as though she were in a long, dark tunnel.

JENNY FELT THE TEARS STARTING IN HER EYES.

*So many memories.*

She laid the shawl on the bed and looked through the other boxes. There were several of her mother's belongings, which she arranged on the dresser and the dressing table—the ivory-handled brush Reuben had given Jerusha to brush out her beautiful golden hair, the small handkerchiefs with the initial J. Jenny sighed and wondered, just for a moment, if this had been the right thing to do.

She took a deep breath and decided it was time to stop mooning about and go unpack her own things. She went down the hall to her room. Boxes were scattered about and several dresses on hangers lay on the bed.

*The difference between my mama and me. She was always so ordered, so meticulous. It was the reason she could sit for hours and stitch those tiny perfect stitches into her wonderful quilts. And me?*

Jenny smiled to herself.

*Look at this mess! Just like when I tried to quilt.*

Another memory came to her. She was nineteen, sitting with her mother and trying her best to learn to quilt. Instead of going into the material, the sharp needle went into the tip of her finger...

*"DU SCHLECHT'R!"*

*"Jenny Springer! You should not say such bad words! You should be ashamed."*

*Jenny's face burned as she reached behind the quilting frame with her left hand and pushed the errant needle through the quilt to complete her stitch. The finger of her other hand, showing a tiny red drop where she had pricked herself, went into her mouth. She stared angrily at the quilt she was working on. The design was awkward, with puckered edges on the pattern pieces where she had attempted to sew them together.*

*"Oh, Mama, I will never, ever be a quilter like you. I just can't do it."*

*Her mother's shocked expression softened somewhat, and she put her arm around the girl's shoulder. "Quilting is a gift from God, and it's true that you don't yet seem to have the eye for it. But you're gifted in so many other ways. Don't be disheartened. Sometimes you're a little* eigensinnig und ungeduldig, *and these qualities do not fit well with quilting. You must learn to still your heart and calm the stream of thoughts rushing through your head." Jerusha enfolded the girl in her arms.*

*"Are you ever sorry that you got me instead of Jenna, Mama?" Jenny whispered.*

*Jerusha paused before replying. "Gott gave me Jenna, and then Gott gave you to me, my dearest. Jenna was a wonderful little girl, and Gott blessed your papa and I beyond measure by giving her to us. When she died, we didn't know how we would ever go on with our lives. But Gott in His mercy sent us a wonderful child to fill the emptiness in our hearts. That child was you. Sorry? No, my darling, I will never be sorry that you came to us. There will always be a place in my heart for Jenna, but now I have you to love and hold. I couldn't hope for a better* dochter.*"*

JENNY TURNED TO HER WRITING DESK, THE ONE HER PAPA MADE for her.

*This house is so full of memories. Maybe I should do some writing and get the ghosts out of my head.*

She went to the box that held Undie, her old Underwood typewriter, lifted it out, and placed it on the desk. She ran her hand over the smooth birch wood of the desk's surface.

*Such a beautiful piece. Papa poured his heart into this. Amish girls rarely become writers, but then Amish men don't usually win the Congressional Medal of Honor like Papa did. I guess we Springers were not your usual Amish family.*

She ran her hand over the knobs on the drawers, looked at the shelf that held her pencils and paper...

She noticed something. Under the shelf was a row of hand-carved flowers all along the back.

*Those flowers. They look like...*

She looked closer.

*Roses!*

Then she remembered the key in her pocket. She pulled it out.

*Jenny. Rose lock.*

She wondered... She began pushing at the little flowers. One, two... the third one moved on a pin and rotated up. There was a hole behind it, narrow, like...

*A key hole!*

She slipped the key into the hole and turned. There was a click and a small drawer slid out of the back of the desk. Inside was something white.

*An envelope!*

Jenny pulled it out. On the envelope, in her father's strong handwriting, was the notation, *Jenny — 1983.*

*This is strange. I'm lost in my memories and then I get a letter from Papa...*

## 5

# NUMBER THREE

ieutenant Elbert Wainwright sat staring at the letter on his desk. Same crooked all cap handwriting.

"TO ANY COP IN WOOSTER — BECAUSE THERE ARE NO SMART ONES!"

Elbert's finger went to the intercom button and pushed. Gary answered. "Linden."

"Detective, come on down. We got another one."

In a few minutes, Detective Linden was by his desk. They stared down at the note.

YA SNOOZE YA LOSE. WHEN I SEND A LETTER YOU PROBABLY SHOULD HAVE ALREADY BEEN RESPONDING. YOU DON'T THINK I'M GOING TO SIT AROUND WAITING FOR YOU TO CATCH UP, DO YOU? NEXT ONE SOON, NUMBER THREE, I'LL LET YOU KNOW. 3 X 3

Gary shook his head in amazement. "This guy is a full-blown psycho."

Elbert looked up. "Have the newspapers started putting

this together? Have you released any information about the similarities?"

"No, Lieutenant. We've got a couple of inquiring reporters who are trying to push us into giving them the scoop, but as far as the public is concerned, these are just two random killings."

Elbert got up and started pacing. Finally, he spoke. "I can tell you if he gets to number three, some wise guy in the press corps will start putting two and two together, or should I say three and three." He sat down again. "So, what do we have from the crime scenes?"

Gary pulled out a notebook. "Not a lot. A couple of cigarette butts outside the preschool in the same spot, like someone had been standing and waiting. We are testing for DNA samples now. A tire track by the side of the road just down from where Anna Myerson parked her bike. We took a cast. A boot track next to it. We cast that as well." He flipped to the next page. "Then we have pieces of the duct tape the killer used to bind their hands behind them and tape their mouths shut, plus the hog-tie rope. We've tested for finger-prints, but nothing. The killer most likely wore gloves."

"And if you find some DNA on the cigarettes. Detective?"

"We have already alerted the National DNA Database people that we might have samples for them to run. We have put out some bulletins and posted some flyers, you know, low key to keep the buzz down."

"And the bulletins said...?"

"Anyone who was in the vicinity of the Buckle My Shoe Preschool on August 10, or at Grosjean Park that may have seen anything suspicious or seen anyone acting suspiciously, let the local police know..."

"Yeah? Any response?"

Gary looked down. "No."

"Have you put the word out on the street, let our snitches and informers know?"

"Well..."

Elbert smiled and got up. "Get your coat, Detective. It's time for a crash course in Gumshoe Police Work 101."

---

GARY LINDEN GOT A PROPER EDUCATION THAT DAY. ELBERT took him to places he had only heard vague rumors about when he was growing up in the Wooster area, even after he had joined the force. Places where you had to walk through alleys and down hidden stairs, smoke-filled rooms above bars, houses of ill-repute and more. Gary followed Elbert in a daze as they went from place to place, looking for answers. And it was always the same. Nobody had heard anything or seen anything. Finally, they stopped at a restaurant.

Gary stared at Elbert in amazement across the table. "You know a lot of people, some real unsavory characters. How in the world..."

Elbert looked at Gary's face and laughed. "I told you I was a uniform a lot longer than most. I walked the beat for ten years. Some of these folks I put in jail, but a lot of them, I helped in some way." He saw the shocked look. "No, I didn't tear up any tickets or get them out of jail if they were guilty, but if they really needed help and they were straight about it, I did what I could. I got known as a cop who would be square with you and give a guy a fair shake. It helped when I needed a hand."

"But some of these people are real criminals."

"Yes, and if I catch them at it, I put them away. That's the deal."

Elbert stared at his cup of coffee. "The strange thing is,

there is nothing on the street, not a whisper. Usually if there is a noteworthy crime like a murder or a big robbery, somebody has heard about it. Crooks are arrogant. They like to brag about their big jobs. So usually there is a snitch who's willing to tell what they know in return for a few bucks. But today, nothing. It's as though our killer doesn't even live in this state."

WHEN THEY GOT BACK TO THE STATION AFTER DINNER, THERE was another letter waiting on Elbert's desk, addressed to ELBERT AND GARY — GOOSE CHASERS, in the now-familiar bold print. Elbert slit it open carefully and read the note.

HI BOYS. YOU BEEN LOOKIN' FOR LOVE IN ALL THE WRONG PLACES. I SEE YOU BUT YOU DON'T SEE ME. PLAYING WITH YOU IS FUN, BUT NOW IT'S TIME FOR NUMBER THREE. 3 X 3.

IT WAS 10:00 P.M. ELBERT AND GARY HAD BEEN PUZZLING over the note for several hours. They had made no progress when Gary thought of something.

"Did you know *Lookin' For Love* is a song? Johnny Lee recorded it around 1980."

Elbert nodded. "Yeah?"

"I'm a little embarrassed to admit this, but I have that song on a Country and Western compilation CD."

Elbert looked up at Gary. "You listen to cowboy music?"

"Well, my dad moved here from Texas. He used to tell us

there are only two kinds of real music... Country and West-ern. So, I grew up listening to a lot of it."

"What are the lyrics?"

Gary furrowed his brow. "Let me see...

*Well, I spent a lifetime lookin' for you*
*Single bars and good time lovers were never true*
*Playin' a fool's game, hopin' to win*
*And tellin' those sweet lies and losin' again.*
*I was lookin' for love in all the wrong places*
*Lookin' for love in too many faces*
*Searchin' their eyes, lookin' for traces*
*Of what I'm dreamin' of*

Elbert perked up. "Singles bars. The song is talking about lonely hearts club watering holes."

Gary shook his head. "There must be at least twenty in the Wooster area alone."

Elbert grinned. "And you would know because...?"

Gary felt his face burning, and he knew he had turned bright red. "Well, I... you see, I was just..."

Elbert chuckled. "Being a cop can get lonely. I know all about that. But our killer is referring to a specific bar. It's almost as if he's dangling it in front of our noses." He looked back at the note. "Okay, it's all right here. Singles bars, a fool's game, can't see him."

The penny dropped for Gary. "There's a bar in Craigton. It's twenty minutes from here. Midge's Fool's Paradise. It's an upscale singles bar."

Elbert looked puzzled. "What's the connection?"

Gary laid it out. "You gave me the idea. Can't see him. A 'Can't-See-Um' is a tiny fly, a midge. We got the singles bar and the reference to a fool's game. It's got to be the place."

"Now you're thinking like a cop. Let's go."

THE DRIVER OF THE WHITE VAN WATCHED THROUGH THE window as Gary and Elbert pulled into the parking lot at Midge's bar.

*Good boys. Almost got here on time.*

There was a whimper from the back of the van. The driver turned. "Not much longer, Missy dear."

SHE WAS TRUSSED UP LIKE THE OTHERS. HER BODY LAY PARTLY in a ditch along the road about two hundred yards from Midge's. The flashing blue and red lights of the police cars lit the yellow tape surrounding the scene and the sequins on her unbuttoned waitress blouse in a kaleidoscopic display.

Gary looked at her sadly. "So young, so pretty. What a waste. Got a name?"

"Missy Berringer. She's a waitress at Midge's. She went off shift around seven and stepped outside. She never came back for her stuff."

Elbert gritted his teeth. "Every murder is a waste, but this guy is a waste of oxygen. We are going to catch him and I am going to be there when they stick that needle in his arm."

The police forensics team was going over every inch of the ground around the site and the doctor was taking pictures. The familiar duct tape bound the girl's hands behind her back and covered her mouth. The orange and black rope looped around her neck and held her legs up behind her back. Elbert and Gary were watching the doctor do his examination. Just then a uniformed cop approached Elbert with an elderly lady in tow.

"We may have caught a break, Lieutenant."

"How so?"

"This is Mrs. Walton. She lives across the road and down about fifty yards. She was looking out her window last night and saw a white van pull into the spot where they found the body. It was only there for about a minute. Someone got out, but she couldn't see them. She heard the back door slam and then the driver's side door shut and the van took off. It passed her house going fast."

Elbert turned to the woman and nodded. "Mrs. Walton. Is there anything else you can remember? Did you see the license plate?"

The woman nodded her head up and down. "Well, officer..."

"Lieutenant."

"Yes, of course. Well, I saw the license plate, but not all of it. There's a streetlight across the road from my house. They put it there a few years ago because there are houses along here and a lot of Midge's customers were leaving the bar drunk. Now, I'm a member of MADD and me and a bunch of my friends went down to that meeting... the city council, you know... oh this must have been four years ago... and we talked to that bunch..."

"That's fine, Mrs. Walton, but let's get back to the license plate. You saw it?"

"Yes, officer..."

"Lieutenant."

"Yeah, sorry. Well, I didn't see the whole plate, but I saw some of it."

"Can you remember that part?"

"Yes, the last two letters. R and Y."

"Are you sure?"

"Perfectly. My husband, who passed away last year... he was walking along the road right over there and just dropped dead. Dangdest thing. They didn't know what killed him, but I was pretty sure it was the bottles of Jack Daniels he kept under the hay mound. He didn't know I knew about that..."

Elbert looked at Gary. "I'm sorry to hear about that, Mrs. Walton, but what about your husband and the license plate?"

"Well, that's easy. My husband's name was Ray. Ray Walton. Same last name as mine, of course, we was married fifty-two years."

Gary interjected. "Ray?"

"Yes, so I remembered the R and the Y. I thought to myself that if there was an A in between them, it would spell 'Ray.' I thought for a minute he was trying to send me a message from beyond, but I don't really go in for that superstitious stuff. It's bad luck to be superstitious."

Gary snorted and turned his head. Mrs. Walton looked at him sharply. "What?"

"Nothing, Mrs. Walton. Go on. Can you remember anything else about the van?"

"Yes, it was a white Chevy cargo van. Ray used to have one. He delivered eggs and meat from our farm to locals in town. And it must have been a few years old because there was a patch of the white paint missing off the side."

"A peeler," Elbert muttered.

"What?"

"A peeler. Back in 1997 or 1998, some environmental groups convinced General Motors to change their primer to a more environmentally friendly paint. It may have been good for the earth, but the cars they painted with it peeled their paint jobs off like a snake in molting season. They had a big class action suit. So, that lets us know it's a white 1998 to

2004 Chevy delivery van with the last letters on the plate RY."

He turned to Mrs. Walton. "That's good, Mrs. Walton, very observant. I wish all my witnesses were as clear on what they saw. Now the officer will take your information and if we need anything more, we will contact you. Here's my card."

The lady glanced at the card. "Thank you..." she glanced down... "Lieutenant."

"Good. Now, if you'll just go with him, we have some more to do here."

"Okay, officer. Anything you need. I may recall some other things. I'm very observant. My friends all say I should have been a detective. Why, once I won a contest..."

"That's fine, Mrs. Walton. Our office will take your information." He turned away as the officer took Mrs. Walton by the arm and led her away. Gary and Elbert turned back to the body. The doctor was just finishing.

"Same cause of death, Lieutenant. Strangulation. But I think he must have tied her up first because there are chafe marks on her ankles and neck where she struggled. Wonder why he changed his M.O?"

"What about his calling card?"

"Let's look."

The doctor finished unfastening the knots in the rope and released the girl's legs. He straightened them and then rolled her over on her back. The front of her blouse was bloody. The doctor spread the blouse open. The girl was not wearing a bra. Blood had run down and dried all the way to the waist of her skirt. Just below her collarbone in the hollow of her chest was the now familiar mark.

3 X 3.

6

## SUSPECTS

ieutenant Elbert Wainwright stared down at the local paper spread out on his desk. Splashed across the front page was a picture. It was a picture of the killer's signature, 3 X 3, scrawled with something red and dripping on a plain piece of paper. Underneath it was a note in the now-familiar handwriting.

ASK THE COPS WHAT THIS HAS TO DO WITH THE THREE RECENT MURDERS IN THE WOOSTER AREA. 3 X 3.

Elbert gritted his teeth. The intercom buzzed. It was Charlene.

"Mal Worthington from the Daily Record on the line, Lieutenant."

Elbert sighed. "Tell Mr. Worthington I am busy and I will get back to him."

By that afternoon, calls flooded the station—the mayor, the sheriff, more reporters, the head of the Chamber of Commerce, the anchor from WQKT evening news... plus a not too friendly interview with his boss, the Chief of Police.

Elbert knew he had to do something before the fire spread. He called Gary and told him to bring everything he had to his office. In a few minutes, Gary came in with a large cardboard box and his notepad.

"I saw that article in the paper. Our guy beat us to the punch and put out the info to get everyone worked up. Or just to get his name in the papers."

"That's right, Detective. Now I've got everyone crawling down my back. The chief is going to release a statement at a press conference. So, we need to give him some ammo. What do we have?"

"Okay, we got some DNA from the cigarette butt, and the National DNA database ran a search. No matches so far. I also have our computer nerds running a search in the Ohio license plate database for any plates with RY in them. It's a laborious process, but my guy says we should eventually get some matches."

The intercom buzzed.

"Yeah, Charlene."

"The evening paper is here. I think you should see it."

"Bring it in."

Charlene brought in the paper and laid it on the desk. The headline was big and bold.

*3 X 3 Murders Rock Wooster!*

The subhead read, "*Do we have a serial killer loose in Wayne County?*"

Elbert shook his head. "The chief will not like this. Okay, I'll write a report and you get back on the plate search. And tomorrow morning, I want you to visit every farm supplier in the area with a sample of that rope and some of the duct tape."

ELBERT STOOD BESIDE HIS CHIEF IN FRONT OF SEVERAL LOCAL news reporters. There were also reporters from Associated Press and behind them the CNN cameras had their red lights on. Several of the reporters had shouted questions when Chief Jarvis came in, but he waved them to silence. Then he read a brief statement.

"There have been three murders in the Wooster area within the last month. The first murder seemed an isolated incident. There were certain clues and identifiers left at the crime scene, but we did not release them to the public because we never do when there is an ongoing investigation. It was only when we found similar identifiers at the scene of the second murder that we realized we might have more than just a random crime on our hands. The third murder confirmed our fear that the same person is responsible for all three killings. We have put our top investigative team on this and are currently pursuing several leads. At the present time, we have no persons of interest in the crime, but we are working hard to bring this perpetrator to justice." The chief looked over at Elbert with a glint in his eye. "Now I am turning the microphone over to Lieutenant Elbert Wainwright, who is our chief investigator on this case. He will take your questions."

Elbert did not miss the grim look on the chief's face.

*And Elbert gets thrown to the wolves...*

He stepped up to the podium and immediately the hands went up and voices stabbed at him in a hubbub of sound.

"Lieutenant Wainwright..." "Lieutenant Wainwright..."

"Lieutenant Wainwright..."

"Lieutenant Wainwright..."

Elbert lowered his hands, palms down, to quiet them and then pointed to an older man in the front row. "Mal."

"Mal Worthington, Daily Record. Lieutenant Wainwright, what can you tell us about the 3 X 3 killer's signature? Did you find it at all the crime scenes?"

Elbert grimaced. "I cannot give you more than general details about the murder scenes since we are in the middle of the investigation. Someone who is the killer or at least familiar with the case sent the picture you all have seen to the newspapers. However, to discourage copycats and pranksters, we cannot tell you how we discovered this so-called signature or what relationship it has to the three murder scenes." Elbert pointed to a young woman who was waving her hand. "Yes?"

"Linda Gehring, Cleveland 19 news. What can you tell us about the victims?"

"Thank you, Linda. We have three women victims, but we are not releasing any names or details until we can investigate any persons of interest who might have something in common with them, or are connected to them. What I can tell you is that, as far as we can determine, there seems to be no connection between any of the victims."

Another hand. "Yes?"

"John Arland, CNN local bureau. Lieutenant, does Ohio have a serial killer on its hands? Another Son of Sam?"

Elbert shook his head. "I'm not willing to say that yet, John, although there is definitely a pattern here. We have some pertinent leads that we are following and the investigation is moving in the right direction. We will give you more information when we have it. Thank you very much, ladies and gentlemen." Elbert turned and walked away from the podium, ignoring the rest of the shouted questions from the press.

Detective Gary Linden climbed back into his car. This was the eighth farm supply story he had visited. They each had obliged him by searching their computers for details in their order history. So far, he had a list of twenty people who had purchased that brand of rope within a ten-day period. Now he only had to visit six more stores.

*Lunch. I need some lunch.*

As he sat at a lunch counter in a local diner, he had an idea. He called into the station and asked for his sergeant. Bill Cowper answered the phone.

"Cowper."

"Yeah, Bill, this is Gary. Can I get you to do something for me? It concerns the murders."

"Sure, Detective. How can I help?"

"Can you search for any grocery stores or gas stations in the locality of the three murders? Say within a twelve-block area?"

"Sure, Gary. But it's gonna take me several hours."

"That's okay, I'll be done with the farm stores by this afternoon and you can give me the list when you get back to the station."

"See you soon."

---

Gary sat at his desk. He had the final list from the farm suppliers. It had the names of forty-five people who bought the orange and black polyester rope and paid for it with a credit card or a check over a ten-day period. Of course, that left out the people who may have paid cash. The duct tape was a little more difficult, but what he was looking for was a match—someone who bought the rope and the tape at the same time. The intercom buzzed. "Linden."

"Yeah, Detective, Bill Cowper. I have that list for you. I have twenty-two gas stations, stores, and quick-marts in those areas. What are we looking for?"

"See if any of those locations have a security camera and if they do, I want to see the tapes from August 10, August 17 and August 23. I'm looking for a white Chevy delivery van with RY in the plate number. Maybe it came in and got caught on a camera at one of the stores or gas stations."

"Okay, I'll get on it."

After Bill's call, Gary went back to work matching up names with purchases using the credit card information. At the end of an hour, he had six people that bought both the rope and duct tape on the same day. All but one bought them at the same store. One person bought the tape and the rope at two different stores.

*Narrowing it down.*

Gary looked at the six names on his list. Jonas Peterson, Randall Kirchner, Will Smethhurst, Bobby Kibler, Laurie Walters and Steven Lambright. He started matching the names with police records on his computer. Peterson had two speeding tickets and a DUI, which he had expunged from his record after two years. He had gone through all the steps and petitioned the court, and now his record was clean. Randall Kirchner was eighty-four years old. Gary did not figure him to be active enough to hog-tie three women after strangling them. Will Smethurst's record showed that he had a concealed carry permit issued by Wayne County and that he was a private detective.

*If he had a gun, he didn't need to strangle them.*

Gary set that one aside. Bobby Kibler. Gary looked at the picture.

*I know him.*

Bobby Kibler was a well-known Wooster coach of the

local High School basketball team and a former all-confer-ence guard at Indiana University when Larry Bird played there. He was often featured as a guest on the local sports program for basketball insights.

*Not a chance Bobby is our guy.*

Laurie Walters was out, and that left Stephen Lambright. A local handyman, no police record, vet. But nothing to say he was not 3 X 3 either.

I guess I'll wait until I see what Bill comes up with.

LATER THAT EVENING, BILL COWPER CALLED. "I PICKED UP tapes from eighteen of the locations that had security cameras. Most of them run on a monthly cycle—they record for a month, file the recording and start a new one. None of the stores use VHS anymore, they record on DVDs. The rest of them did not have a camera."

"Which means we have to sit through eighteen weeks, times three, looking for our white van. As the guy said in Jaws, 'we're gonna need a bigger boat'."

Bill laughed. "I can get some guys to help us go through them. Many hands make light work."

"Okay, Bill, you get the guys and I'll pull some recorders together. Let's meet at the station at 10:00 a.m. tomorrow."

"See you then."

# 7

# LETTER FROM THE PAST

*J*enny stared at the envelope. *Jenny—1983.*

*That's the year my mama and papa died. Papa made this desk for me when I started writing, just a few months before the accident...*

She picked up a letter opener and carefully slit the envelope open. Inside was a single page with a handwritten note from Reuben.

*My dearest Jenny,*

*Just a note to let you know how much I love you and how much building this desk for you means to me. I could not be prouder of you.*

*You have a splendid gift for writing. I hope this desk will help you on that journey. I will always remember how Gott brought you to us and how much happiness your life has given to us and to others. And how, from that little lost girl that came into our hearts, you have grown into the remarkable woman you are.*

*In the days ahead, I hope you will look back on the things of the past with joy and not sorrow. I look for the day that you will truly find peace again in your life.*

*Papa*


THE MEMORIES CAME AGAIN—OF HER PAPA AND MAMA AND this house.

*This is the second time I've come home...*

Jenny thought back to the time that she had moved from Pennsylvania the first time, after Jonathan had disappeared at sea and everyone gave him up for dead. She came to stay at the old house with Reuben and Jerusha, because it was just too hard being alone in Pennsylvania. It had been the hardest time in her life. She thought she would never get over losing Jonathan and then one day...


*Then came a day when Jenny awoke to a soft dawn that crept into her room like a mischievous child, softly kissing her awake with the delicate touch of a rose-colored morning. Jenny opened her eyes and saw the pale colors blushing in the fresh sky. She rose, wrapped a shawl around her shoulders, and slipped outside. The day was fresh and clean and warm, and the grass felt cool and damp against her bare feet. Above her head, the plum trees were just sprouting the tiny pink buds that would soon burst into brilliant color and paint the world with God's palette. A single wren twittered its call, and stillness lay on the land.*

*Jenny's heart stirred within her at the unexpected beauty of the morning. An old barn cat came around the side of the house, meowed loudly, and bunted her head against Jenny's leg. Jenny smiled and reached down to scratch the cat behind the ears.*

"Hello, Perticket."

*The old cat stayed for a moment, enjoying the attention, and then wandered off. Jenny took a deep breath, and the fresh air* tasted sweet. The sun peeked up over the hills to the east, and bright rays of sun shining through the trees cast easy shadows across the fields. A little breeze sprang up, and the air stirred around her, gently lifting the curls from her face. Above her, a formation of Canadian geese flew north, honking as they went. The wonder of the day touched Jenny's senses, and a thought rose in her heart like a small trout rising for a fly in a still mountain lake.

*I'm still alive. This didn't kill me, and I can still find joy and wonder in a day.*

The screen door creaked behind her, and she looked around to see her papa coming out on the porch. He was dressed for work, and his handsome face broke into a smile. Reuben stepped down from the porch and came over to Jenny.

"You have a glow about you this morning, *dochter.* It's good for my heart to see life creeping back into you."

Jenny stepped into the circle of Reuben's arms.

*Yes, I do feel life coming back into me. It's as though I am raised from the dead!*

"Papa, thank you!"

"For what, Jenny?"

"For not giving up on me, for walking beside me, and for being my rock when the storm raged most fiercely about me."

Reuben's arms tightened around her. Then he spoke, and she could tell the words were difficult by the way they seemed to be pulled from him, syllable by syllable.

"When our Jenna died, I wanted to die too. I felt so helpless, and I believed that but for my wrongheadedness, Jenna would have lived. If *das Vollkennen des Gottes* hadn't sent someone to help me, I would have died by my own hand. And then *Gott,* in His infinite mercy and grace, sent you to us. I can't explain how it happened, but when I saw you for the first time, I knew you belonged to me and to your mama forever. I knew *Gott* gave me a *second chance, and I loved you with every bit of the love I had for Jenna. And so, when I see you suffer, I suffer too."*

*Jenny looked into her papa's eyes, the deep sea-blue eyes with the smile behind them, and saw home and safety in them.*

*"And I would do anything to see you happy again. You make* sonnenschein in meinem Herzen. *And now you have given us Rachel, and the joy she brings with her is beyond our understanding. I can't give Jonathan back to you. If I could, I would give my life to do so. But that's beyond me, so I give you my love and this place and whatever you need to be happy again. That's my prayer."*

Jenny looked at the note again.

*He was so worried that I would never be happy again. He left this letter for me as his way of giving me some happiness. But he died before he gave me the key. And now, all these years later, I receive love from my papa.*

A scripture came to her mind.

*O the depth of the riches, both of the wisdom and knowledge of God! How unsearchable are his judgments, and his ways past finding out!*

Tears came unbidden.

Just then, she heard Bobby coming in the back door. She quickly wiped her eyes with a hanky from her pocket and then went out to the kitchen. She had the letter in her hand.

"Look, Bobby. I found this letter inside my old desk. It's from Papa. He wrote it just before he died. It was in a secret drawer he built into the desk, but he never got to give me the key."

Bobby took the note. "How'd you open the drawer?"

"I found the key in the shed. It's been hanging on a nail out there since before I packed their things away. There was a tag that said 'Jenny-Rose Lock'. There are little carved roses along the back under the shelves and behind one of them was a keyhole."

Bobby read the note and then sat down. "This is nice... You know, your dad really loved you. I remember when that crooked bishop from Lancaster slapped you and your dad found out. I wouldn't have given three nickels for his chances of getting out of this town with his face intact. I can just imagine Reuben's eyes when he stared Lapp down."

Jenny smiled. "Yes, I feared for the man too, but Papa kept his composure and let him go without knocking him into next week. I think Lapp had an epiphany—he realized he had crossed a line he never should have gone near. When Papa took hold of his shirt and looked into his eyes, Lapp turned white as a sheet."

Bobby laughed. "Yeah, your dad was an enigma. An Amish man who saved my life and won the congressional medal of honor by holding off a platoon of Japanese soldiers with his bare hands, and yet, the gentlest man I ever met. It's good you found this. It's good when the past can show you how you overcame the hard things in your life. This is a reminder that not everything we go through is painful."

Jenny nodded. "Yes, it's like finding a treasure. The past can tell us a lot."

*Yes, Jenny, the past can tell us a lot.*

"What?"

Bobby looked up. Furrowed his brow. "I didn't say anything."

"You didn't?"

"No, I was reading the note again."

"Odd..."

JENNY SAT IN THE FRONT ROOM WITH BOBBY. THEY HAD finished dinner and Bobby was reading the local paper. He looked up from an article he was reading.

"Looks like our buddy, Elbert, has his hands full."

Jenny looked up from some knitting she was working on. "What do you mean?"

"Have you read anything about these three times three murders?"

Jenny shook her head. "No, what's that?"

"The article says there's a serial killer loose in Wayne County. Someone murdered three women, and it seems the killer leaves a signature—a three, an X, and another three. And he's been sending mocking letters to the police before he commits his crimes. It's created quite a stir in Wooster."

"What else does it say?"

"Well, it says Elbert is the lead investigator," he looked over the top of the paper... "and I'll bet he's under a lot of pressure. A triple murder is a big deal, especially when it's some nut job who's just going around picking victims randomly."

Jenny looked up again. "Well, I've lived in small villages all my life and I can tell you that nothing is truly random, especially crime. People always have a motive, so even when it seems random, there's always something underneath. Sex, money, or power motivate the criminal. So, what may seem to be random is probably well thought out. What else does it say?"

"The usual cover information. Elbert gave an interview and said the police have several leads they are pursuing. That means they have nothing."

"Does it mention the names of the women?"

"Yes, but there are no details until they notify all the next of kin. Let's see... Anna Myerson, Liz Ingersoll, and Missy Berringer."

Jenny shook her head. "Never heard of them. Certainly not Amish names. I guess detective Wainwright won't be calling us on this one."

Bobby looked up again. "Elbert's not a detective anymore. He's a lieutenant. Seems like the two big cases he solved earned him a promotion. Too bad there's not a promotion for Amish detectives."

Jenny looked down at her knitting. "I just gave Elbert a few pushes in the right direction."

"Well, you did more than that, Jenny. I seem to remember you and I doing a lot of the groundwork on those cases. And the insights you had opened those cases up. Danny Whitmer would still be staring out the window at the Apple Creek Center if it wasn't for you."

Jenny put her knitting down. "I'm glad Elbert got the recognition. He's a good man, and he worked hard. I'm just an aging Amish woman who knows a lot of the people around Apple Creek. I'm glad I could help, but I certainly don't want the glory."

"You mean like when you wrote those books about your family and turned them over to that *Englischer* author?"

Jenny nodded. "The important thing was getting those stories told. Those books are still selling, so many people are learning about the Amish way of life, and I'm not talking about the kind of foolishness they read about in the books they buy at Walmart. The Amish are real people who face real and often desperate situations that only *Gott* can fix. Everything is not peachy keen for the Amish, just because they are Amish. If I can help bring understanding about my people's way of life, then I am perfectly satisfied."

# 8

# DAYLIGHT

*E*lbert Wainwright sat in his office staring out the window. The late August heat wave had dissipated, the temperature dropped and outside a wet drizzle splashed against the windows in his office.

It had been a week since the last murder and the killer was going to stick to his stated agenda.

*He said he was going to kill three women. So now does he just disappear?*

The intercom buzzed. Elbert pressed the button. "Wainwright."

"Lieutenant? Sergeant Cowper here. Gary and I think we may have something. Can we bring some of the material I got from two store cameras down to your office?"

"Sure, Bill. See you in a minute."

In a few minutes, there was a knock and Bill Cowper and Gary Linden came in. Bill carried a DVD player and a small monitor.

"Give us a minute to hook this up, Lieutenant."

Bill went to a long table against the wall, set up the monitor, and quickly hooked it to the player. Gary came over to Elbert's desk.

"I had Bill do a check on all the gas stations and grocery stores in the vicinity of each of the murders—within a ten-block area. He came up with a list of twenty-two stations and quick marts in those areas. When he canvassed them, he found that eighteen of them had security cameras. Most of them ran on a weekly cycle, so they recorded everything in their parking lots for a week, filed it and put in a new disk. We got the owners to let us make copies of all the videos that were within our time-frame. Then we spent yesterday going through them. And I think we found something."

Elbert was interested. "Show me."

Gary nodded, and Bill started the machine. "The first one is from Bob's Stop and Go right down the road from Midge's in Craigton. This was about half an hour before Missy Berringer went missing. A white Chevy delivery van pulls in past the camera and gets some gas. Check the plates."

Elbert went to the table and looked. The plate was fuzzy, but visible. RYB 9194. He nodded.

Bill advanced the player, and the next scene came up. "This is Johnny's In and Out over off Chase street, near the school where Liz Ingersoll was killed. The camera recorded it about forty-five minutes before the murder. You'll see the same van."

Elbert watched. The white Chevy van pulled in, drove past the camera and into a parking space. The plate was clearer in this recording. RYB 9194.

"The guy sat there for about forty minutes and then drove away. If it's our killer, he went straight to the school, killed Ingersoll, and then took off."

"Did you run the plates?"

"Yeah, the van belongs to a guy named Steven Lambright."

Gary spoke up. "But here's the kicker, Lieutenant. I ran through all the records of anyone who bought that orange and black rope and duct tape from the local supply stores and I matched six names that used their credit card to buy the items. One of them was Steven Lambright."

"Did you get an address?"

"Yes, he lives on a farm outside town on Uhl Road." Gary pulled out a piece of paper. "12207 Uhl."

Elbert sat down at his desk and picked up the phone. "Charlene, get me Judge Thatcher."

He waited for a moment, then spoke. "Hello, Judge Thatcher? This is Lieutenant Wainwright. Good, thanks. I need to request a search warrant for a house on Uhl road." He looked up.

Gary read it again. "12207 Uhl."

"Yes, 12207 Uhl. I have probable cause to believe that a person of interest regarding the three times three murders is residing on the property. Sure, I'll write up the affidavit with the pertinent information and bring it right over."

He hung up. Gary was already going out the door. "I'll have it in ten minutes, Lieutenant."

FLASHING RED AND BLUE LIGHTS LIT THE OUTSIDE OF THE white farm house. An officer with a bull horn called out, "Steven Lambright, we have a warrant to search your home. Come out with your hands up."

Suddenly, there was shouting from the back of the house. "Stop where you are or we'll shoot."

There was more hubbub and then two officers came

around the house with a man in tow, his hands handcuffed behind him. He had a terrified look on his face. Elbert went up to him. "Steven Lambright?"

The man nodded. His long unkempt hair was wet with perspiration and hung in lank locks in front of his eyes. He had a three-day growth of beard on his face. He closed his eyes. "The lights... the lights hurt me..."

"Why'd you run, Steven?"

The man looked confused. "I was afraid, the lights and the noise. Am I under arrest?"

"Not yet. We are detaining you temporarily because we have reasonable suspicion to believe that you were involved in criminal activity within the last month in Wayne County."

"But I did nothing."

"Do you own a white Chevrolet delivery van, license number RYB 9194?"

"I did, but I'm pretty sure someone stole it a month ago."

"Uh-huh. We don't have a record of your van being stolen. And if someone stole it, why would the thief hide it behind your barn?"

The man looked around. "I didn't report it because I don't enjoy talking to the police. I figured I just forgot where I left it. I have trouble that way. I get forgetful, you know. But then I never found it, so I figured someone stole it. I was going to report it."

Elbert pointed to the nearest police car. "Stephen Lambright, we have a warrant to search your home and property, so I want you to sit in the back of this vehicle until we finish." Elbert turned to Gary and Bill. "Okay, guys. I want you to go over this place with a fine-tooth comb."

"You got it, Lieutenant."

AN HOUR LATER, GARY CAME UP TO ELBERT. "LIEUTENANT, you need to see this." He led the way to the decrepit barn behind the house. They went inside and Gary took Elbert over to the back wall. He held up a piece of weathered board.

"We were checking the walls, and this board moved. We took it off and found this in the space between the joists."

Gary pulled on some latex gloves and then shined a flashlight into the space. At the bottom was a bundle of red and black rope and a roll of duct tape. "We've taken pictures, so I'm going to bring out the evidence." He turned to a forensics guy. "Put some plastic down on that bench, so we keep this stuff clean."

He lifted out the rope and the tape and placed them on the workbench.

"There's something else in there, Detective."

Gary looked again. At the bottom of the space was an envelope. He reached down and carefully lifted it out. It was not sealed, so he opened it. Inside were several pictures. He carefully removed them and placed them on the plastic. The policemen looked down. The pictures were from a polaroid type camera, a little fuzzy but still very graphic. The murderer had taped their mouths but made sure their eyes were open. Their blouses were open and the telltale signature was fully visible. The blood from the fresh wounds ran down the skin of the victims. Gary noticed something. The first two women were obviously dead, their eyes lifeless. Missy Berringer's eyes were wide open, filled with fear. He had marked her when she was still alive.

Gary felt like throwing up. "This guy is really a sicko."

Just then, another cop came into the barn. "Lieutenant, there's a gully down at the back of the property. We were searching it and we found the white van under a pile of brush. The men are still going through it, but we found this right away." The officer held up a polaroid camera in a plastic bag. "There's still film in it."

Elbert walked out to the car where Steven Lambright huddled in the back. He opened the door. "Steven Lambright, we are arresting you on suspicion of the murders of Anna Myerson, Liz Ingersoll, and Missy Berringer. You have the right to remain silent. Anything you say can and will be used against you in a court of law. You have the right to talk to a lawyer for advice before we ask you any questions. You have the right to have a lawyer with you during questioning. If you cannot afford a lawyer, one will be appointed for you before any questioning if you wish. If you decide to answer questions now without a lawyer present, you have the right to stop answering at any time."

Steven Lambright stared up at Elbert, a horrified expression on his face. "But I didn't kill anybody. You got it all wrong."

Elbert nodded. "I must remind you that anything you say may be used against you in a court of law. Do you have anything to tell us?"

"I didn't do it. I didn't kill anyone."

Elbert turned to the officer by the car. "Okay, take him down to the station and book him. Let him make his phone call if he asks for one. I want everything by the book. No slipups. I want an airtight case against this guy, and I don't want any do-gooder attorneys coming in and getting him off on a technicality."

The officer nodded. "You got it, Lieutenant."

Elbert turned to the men gathered around him. "Seal this place off. I don't want anybody in here and especially no members of the press. I want this place examined with a magnifying glass. I want casts taken of the tires on the van, and I want a DNA sample from our suspect when he's booked. Check for cigarettes or anything else that might have DNA in the house. Okay, get to work."

The officers spread out and began their investigative work.

Elbert turned to Gary and Bill. "Good work, Detective, Sergeant. This looks like an open and shut case."

THE NEXT MORNING GARY CAME IN TO ELBERT'S OFFICE. HE had some pictures in his hand. "Lieutenant, we got a match on the tire tracks found at the Park and down the road from the Walton house. It was the white van all right. And we found a couple of ashtrays full of butts in the house. We are matching the DNA on them to the sample we took from the suspect and the DNA from the butt we found at the crime scene. We got this guy. Oh, and he got his phone call."

"Did he lawyer up?"

"Nope, he called his mother."

Elbert smiled. "You know, Detective, there may be some hope for you yet."

LATER THAT AFTERNOON, ELBERT GOT A BUZZ ON THE intercom. He had been sitting at his desk, feeling vaguely smug and satisfied with himself. He fingered the button. "Yes, Charlene?"

"There's a woman to see you, Detective. It's Steven Lambright's mother."

"Show her in, Charlene."

The door opened and Charlene came in. She turned and

motioned to someone outside. "Come in, Mrs. Lambright. The lieutenant is very nice. He won't hurt you."

A woman put her head in the door. A white *kappe,* plain blue dress... Elbert had seen that kind of clothing before. Steven Lambright's mother was Amish!

Elbert stood up. "Come in, Mrs. Lambright, come in." He pointed to a chair in front of his desk. "Sit here. Can I get you anything, coffee, tea?"

The woman sank down in the chair, then shook her head. "*Nein, danke.*"

Elbert sat back down. "What can I do for you, Mrs. Lambright?"

The woman paused...

"Don't be afraid, Mrs. Lambright, just tell me."

She nodded. "*Ja, ja,* I heard you are good with the Amish, so I will say what I have to say. It's about my son. He is not a murderer. He is, what do you say... disabled."

"In what way Mrs. Lambright?"

"He was in the war, in Vietnam. He has, they call it PTSD?"

"Yes, post-traumatic stress disorder."

"*Ja,* we say *Posttraumatische Belastungsstörung.*"

"I thought the Amish did not believe in war, Mrs. Lambright."

She shook her head and Elbert caught a glint of a tear in her eye. "Steven went away from our faith a long time ago. When he was on *Rumspringa...* you know this *Rumspringa?*"

"Yes. That's when the Amish kids get to try out being in the regular world."

"*Ja, die Englischer welt.* Steven came home one night during his *Rumspringa.* He was terrified. He gathered up some clothes as fast as he could and left. I found out later from a letter that he enlisted in the army over in Indianapolis. He left for basic training within two days and I never saw him until he came home wounded from the Tet offensive. When he came home, he was broken. He was not my Steven. He has been in and out of hospitals for years. He cannot remember anything that happened to him before he was in that battle. He has horrible dreams. He is very changed except for one thing."

"What's that, Mrs. Lambright?"

"When he saw the killing, when he killed men in Vietnam and saw his friends dying horribly, he knew Jesus was right, that men should not kill each other. When he came home on leave, He swore to me he would leave the army and never kill again. He ran away, but they caught him. Steven refused to go back and, except they knew he was sick, they would have put him in prison. He was in a VA hospital instead. He was there, off and on, for over twenty-five years. So, I know this about my son. He would kill no one."

# 9

# CALL FOR HELP

It was mid-September, and the trial of Steven Lambright was moving quickly. The state assigned Lambright a pro-bono defense attorney, but there was not a lot the woman could do. She was young, and unfamiliar with the tricks and tools of a high-profile murder defense. She was basing her defense on Lambright's mental condition, but the chances the plea would work were iffy at best.

Elbert Wainwright met Gary Linden outside the courtroom during a short recess on the trial's fourth day.

"How'd your testimony go, Detective?"

"Piece of cake, Lieutenant. The prosecutor walked me through step by step—the DNA on the cigarette butts, tire tracks, the van in the woods, the tape and rope, trying to flee —this guy is going to get a hot shot if the defense can't get the jury to buy a mental plea."

"Well, I feel sorry for the poor kid that's defending him. Just out of law school, working for a public defender, and she gets the biggest trial in the last ten years. And Lambright is not the most communicative client. If he keeps up the oddball approach, he just may swing a trip to the nuthouse."

Gary looked around. "Have you seen his mother today?"

Elbert nodded. "Yes, she's been here every day. There's been several folks from the Amish community here with her. She is absolutely convinced that her son is innocent. She says he swore never to kill again after he fought in the Tet offensive in Nam and went through some brutal stuff, and she believes him."

Gary shook his head. "The guy would say anything to get off. He knows he's about to get his ticket punched."

Elbert was silent for a minute. "All the same, I kind of wish Jenny Hershberger was around. I'd like to get her sense of this whole deal, being how the Amish community is getting so involved."

Just then, Elbert felt a tug on his arm. He turned to find Mrs. Lambright looking up at him. He put on his 'official business' face.

"Good morning, Mrs. Lambright. How may I help you?"

Mrs. Lambright was a tiny woman, but Elbert could sense a determination about her, something in her eyes and the set of her jaw.

"You're railroading an innocent man, Lieutenant."

Elbert sighed. "Now look, Mrs. Lambright, you've been here every day. You've heard the evidence. They have Steven's DNA samples from the scene of the crime. They have tire tracks that match his van, and they found the rope and the duct tape used in the murders in Steven's barn. It's an open and shut case. What we call a perfect storm of evidence."

"A little too perfect, don't you think, Detective? I agree things do not look *gut* for *meine kind*. But the one thing you will not believe is why this whole thing is wrong."

"What's that, Mrs. Lambright?"

"When he came back from Vietnam, Steven swore he would never kill again. And Steven, though he has done some bad things in his life, has never, ever, lied to me."

Elbert shook his head. "You know that, but I don't, Mrs. Lambright. Now you'll have to excuse me." Elbert turned to walk away.

She called after him. "You are convicting an innocent man, Lieutenant. My Steven is innocent. You should think about that before you go to sleep, if you can sleep."

THAT NIGHT ELBERT COULD NOT SLEEP. HE KEPT HAVING A weird, crazy nightmare that brought him to the edge of consciousness without ever waking him up. Amish men with guns were chasing him through dark streets, their long beards twisting and curling in the wind. It was raining, and he made a turn in the dark and ran down an alleyway that dead-ended at a brick wall. Painted on the wall in dripping red paint—or was it blood—was the now familiar 3 X 3 signature. He turned and ran back to the street. Now the Amish men had military rifles and were coming down the street after him. His legs were frozen, like he was stuck in knee-deep mud. He couldn't move. They were closer now, but then, just as they got to him, they went all fuzzy and turned into Asian men in uniforms. They were North Vietnamese! Now they were shouting at him in a language he didn't understand and then someone was running beside him — it was Steven Lambright. Steven was shouting something too... "Don't let them get you... they'll kill you like I killed them... I won't go back... Jesus was right... you shouldn't kill... you should not kill..." They ran and ran and the Vietnamese soldiers turned back into Amish men, but now they did not have guns, only pitchforks and hay rakes. They were screaming at him... thou shall not kill... thou shall not kill...

Elbert woke up. It was very early in the morning, the gray light of dawn edging the hills to the east. He sat up in bed and took deep breaths, gasping. Sweat poured down his face. He sat for a long time, trying to catch his breath. When he calmed down, he flopped back on the pillow and stared up at the ceiling.

*Wow! That was crazy.*

Elbert turned his head slowly and looked over at the alarm clock. Six o'clock. He turned over in the bed and tried to calm his mind. That lasted about twenty minutes, and then he knew he had to get up. He looked at the clock. Six twenty. Then he had an idea.

*It's almost seven thirty in Pennsylvania. I bet Jenny is already up.*

He reached for his phone, but paused.

*I'll give her twenty minutes.*

He swung his legs over the side of the bed, put his feet into his slippers, and stood up. His robe was on the chair by the bed. He slipped it on, tied it around him, and headed for the kitchen. The morning sun was coming in the window and it took a minute for his eyes to adjust. He opened the cupboard, got the jar of coffee beans out, and spooned five measuring cups into the grinder. Then he put some water into the coffee carafe and poured it into the coffee pot. Hot, bold, go. The smell of the fresh ground beans as the hot water hit them woke him up a bit. In a minute, the coffee was brewing. In ten minutes, it was done, and he poured himself a cup. Half and half from the refrigerator. Then he sat down and waited until the clock hit the hour.

*Okay, I'll call her.*

Elbert looked at the contact list on his phone and dialed the familiar number. He waited for a few seconds and then a familiar voice came on.

"This is Bobby Halverson. I'm retired. Leave a message and I'll get back." There was a pause and then the message beep.

"Bobby, hi. This is Elbert Wainwright. I'm trying to get in touch with Jenny. Can you have her call me?"

Disappointed, he hung up and took another sip of his coffee. He sat staring at the wall, drifting back into the dream. He jerked when the phone rang.

*A bit high-strung, aren't we, Elbert?*

"Wainwright."

"Elbert? This is Bobby Halverson."

Elbert felt himself relax. "Bobby, how are you?"

"I'm great, still above ground and taking nourishment. What's up?"

*Bobby never messes around.*

"I'm looking for Jenny. I've got a tough case on my hands and the Amish are involved. I have a few questions and I thought I could pick her brain."

"Well, why don't you drop by her house and ask her?"

Elbert chuckled. "Yeah, right. Except I don't have time to drive to Pennsylvania."

"No, I'm not kidding. Why don't you drop by her house? She moved back to Apple Creek."

"What?"

"Yep. Her cousin offered to sell her the old house at a great price and she bought it. She's going to be in her old home for a good part of the year."

"What about you? Are you staying out there?"

"Well, no. I've come home, too. I'm just back in Paradise

to pick up a few things and get my dog. I'll be living in the in-law cottage out back. Kind of nice to be back in my old stomping grounds. So, what's the case? Steven Lambright?"

"Yeah, how did you know?"

"I may have been born at night, Elbert, but I wasn't born last night. The 3 X 3 murders are the biggest thing to hit Wayne County, since that crooked bishop, Henry Lapp, was involved in the death of Jenny's parents. We read about Lambright in the papers. Jenny noticed the accused had an Amish name. Not much gets by that girl."

"Did it spark her interest?"

"Like I said, drop on by. You know where her place is. She'll be glad to see you."

"Are you going to be here soon?"

"Yeah, I got a few more days to get everything gathered up and then I'll be coming home. I'm bringing Daniel and Rachel with me."

"Did they move too?"

"No, but Daniel got a job, actually more than a job. He's going partners with a horse breeder over in Millersburg. So, he's going to be in Wayne County a lot. And Rachel and Daniel's boy, Levon, is getting married, so he'll move into the paradise farm and run it. Everything just seemed to fall into place. So, I'd say you better get over to the Springer place. If I know Jenny, she's expecting you. See you soon."

The phone went dead. Elbert stared down at it and shook his head.

*Fell into place. I guess so...*

---

ELBERT PULLED UP THE DRIVEWAY TO JENNY'S HOUSE. GARY Linden sat in the passenger seat.

"Lieutenant, are you sure this is a good idea? Getting an old woman involved in such a big-time murder case?"

Elbert turned to his subordinate. "Jenny Hershberger is not just an old woman. She is the most astute judge of people I have ever met. Because she has lived in small communities her whole life, she knows people, why they do the things they do. She has an incredible insight into human nature. Plus, she is Amish and the Amish community is becoming more and more involved in this case. She is a natural historian, almost like an Irish Shanachie."

"What's that?"

Elbert sighed.

*What do they teach these kids in school?*

"An Irish Shanachie is a storyteller, but their stories are based on the memorized history of their people. A Shanachie can tell stories that go back hundreds of years and if you check them, you find that they perfectly match the handwritten records of the parish priests. That's Jenny Hershberger. She knows the history of her people all the way back to Menno Simons and Jacob Amman. She's written books about it."

"Books? But I thought the Amish could hardly even write. Don't they stop school in the eighth grade?"

"You don't just get knowledge out of books, Detective. This woman has done more living than you or I together. So, mind your manners and keep your ears open."

At that moment, the front door opened, and an Amish woman came out. She walked down the steps and came up to the car. Elbert rolled down the window. Jenny leaned down and smiled.

"Hello Elbert. I was wondering when you would show up. And who's this?"

Elbert looked at Gary's face, now distorted by a big look of surprise.

"This is one of my detectives, Gary Linden."

"Oh yes, you've been working on the Lambright case. Nice to meet you, young man. Well *kumm* in, Elbert. I've got *kaffee und küchen.* I also have some ideas about all this."

Elbert only smiled.

# QUESTIONS

Detective Gary Linden sat on the couch in Jenny's front room. There were oil lamps on the walls and decorative doilies and needlework displayed here and there. The room was comfortable and relaxing. Jenny came in from the kitchen with another tray of sliced cake and the coffeepot. She offered some more cake to Gary, which he slid onto his plate, and then she poured some of the coffee into his cup.

"This cake is delicious, Mrs. Hershberger. This is my third piece. I'm making a pig of myself."

"Jenny, Detective, please call me Jenny."

"Alright… Jenny. Anyhow, the cake is delicious."

Jenny smiled. Even though she was obviously somewhere in her sixties, she had not "decayed" as some older women do. She was still lovely and Gary could tell that her hair had once been red, for a few strands of that color remained among the predominant grey.

"It's my mother's recipe. She was a master at everything she set her hand to—cooking, decorating the house, tending her garden, canning food, but especially quilting. She was a master quilter."

"I thought all Amish women quilted," Gary mumbled through his mouthful of cake.

Jenny laughed, and the sound was charming. "Oh no, Detective, that's not exactly true. I am the world's worst quilter. I couldn't sew a straight line if you paid me."

Elbert nodded. "Yes, but you have many other gifts."

Jenny's face reddened. "You are too kind, Elbert."

Elbert looked over at Gary. "Just for the record, Detective, without the help of this little woman, I would still sit at your desk and you would probably be pounding a beat. Jenny's insights into the two major cases that got me where I am today were extraordinary. And it's because she is interested in every kind of problem that she is such a great detective— the bishop's missing umbrella, why the neighbor's cat got sick, a misplaced package of soup bones—every one of these is grist for her mill. And by the way, it was one of her mother's quilts that helped us solve the mystery of the girl in the box."

Jenny nodded. "In my years living in Apple Creek and Paradise, I have seen that villages are a microcosm of the larger world. The way people behave in your neighborhood is exactly the way they behave out in the world. So, the glaring headlines you read in the paper about horrible crimes actually tell the story of one of your neighbors." She turned to Gary.

"What do you know about the Amish, Detective?"

"Not much, Mrs... uh, Jenny. I didn't grow up around here and only came to Ohio from Texas to go to Ohio State. All I know is they don't drive cars and don't have phones."

Jenny smiled. "Well, Detective, I can see you have a very limited understanding of the Amish, and since Steven

Lambright grew up Amish, it's probably time for you to get an update on his background." She took a breath. "The Amish are not just one group, but they have several, what the *Englisch* might call, denominations."

Gary was puzzled. "*Englisch?*"

Jenny glanced at Elbert and then continued. "Yes, that is the term we use to refer to everyone who is not Amish. It came about because most Amish descend from German or Swiss stock. So, the rest of the world is *Englisch.* Now, like I said, there are several denominations of Amish. The Old Order Amish, which is the primary group of Amish, are distinguished from less conservative groups of Amish by their strict adherence to the practice of forbidding automobile ownership and their traditional manner of dress. Old Order Amish are what many outsiders, *Englischers,* picture when they think of the Amish."

"Like you?"

Jenny smiled. "Yes, I am Old Order Amish. Back in the 1800s, there were a series of conferences that separated the conservatives in my movement from the progressives, who then referred to themselves as Amish Mennonites."

"Kind of like Republicans and Democrats?"

"Not exactly, Detective, but somewhat. The Old Order Amish group ranges from the *Swartzenrüber* and the Nebraska Amish who never use gas-powered tools and tractors, mechanical milking machines, power belts or chain saws, pressurized lamps, or inside flush toilets. However, they do occasionally use motorized washing machines. On the other end of the spectrum is Kalona Iowa Amish who use these things plus owning cars and using phones."

"Wow, I did not know."

"The Amish group I grew up in is somewhere in the middle of the Old Order Amish. We have inside flush toilets and running water, and propane refrigerators. What we try to avoid is being connected."

"Connected?"

"Yes. We avoid being connected to the power grid and if we need electricity, we use generators or, in these modern times, solar panels. As you can see, I don't have any electric lamps, although Bobby has threatened to wire me up for a whole-house generator. I use oil lamps. However, my refrigerator is propane-powered. We don't hook up to the sewer system, but we have septic tanks. And we especially don't connect to the internet or use computers that can be hooked up to it. We want to stay 'disconnected' from the world as much as possible."

"No internet? No computers? How do you find out anything?"

Elbert jumped in. "You know, Detective, there actually was a functioning world before computers came along."

Jenny nodded. "After I finished the eighth grade, my parents, knowing I had a love for study, let me take a job as an intern at the Wooster public library. They had all the books I needed to uncover the history of my people. When I discovered the Biography and Genealogy Master Index, I could trace my ancestors all the way back to Princess Isabella of Poland in the 1500s. When I met my husband, Jonathan Hershberger, I was able to show him he and I were very distant cousins and that his family had originally been Amish. At that time of his life, he was what we called a hippy, and well, in his own words, it 'blew his mind.'"

The phrase was so incongruous coming from Jenny, they all laughed.

"So regarding your case, you have Steven Lambright, who grew up Old Order Amish, but left the faith in his late teens and joined the army."

Now Gary was really puzzled. "But I thought Amish hated war?"

"That is true, we do. We believe Jesus tells us not to kill, and that is one of the guiding principles of our faith. But there is also a great division in our people. Many of our men feel the Amish are not exempt from defending the country that gives them so much freedom in their choice of religion. It's a real conundrum. Should a pacifist take up arms to defend one of the few countries that allows him to be a pacifist? My father went to war and fought as a Marine on Guadalcanal. He won the congressional medal of honor for saving the men of his platoon, including my 'uncle', Bobby Halverson, who was my father's best friend."

"*The* Bobby Halverson? Who used to be sheriff of Wayne County?"

"The same," said Elbert. "Sheriff Halverson has been Jenny's main helper in solving two major crimes that had to do with the Amish community. For which I am very appreciative."

"I heard a lot about him when I was in the police academy. Seems like he was very respected."

"He was a war hero, and a good friend to those on the right side of the law, but he didn't take guff from crooks. Because of his friendship with Jenny's father, he was very respected and trusted by the local Amish. In fact, they often came out to vote for him as sheriff, something they rarely do. You'll be meeting him soon, since he has moved back to Wayne County with Jenny."

Jenny looked at the two policemen. "Tell me what you know about Steven Lambright."

Elbert nodded for Gary to begin.

"This is what I learned about Stephen from his mother. He grew up Amish, but something made him want to get out of town when he was in his late teens. He had gone through, I think she called it Ramspiner or something like that..."

Jenny chuckled. "*Rumspringa.* It's a time in every Amish teen's life when the parents step back and let them go out into the world. We think of it as a rite of passage and in the German language, it literally means 'jumping or hopping around.' It normally begins at sixteen and ends when a youth either is baptized in the Amish faith or leave the community. And by the way, over ninety percent of all Amish youth remain in the faith. However, during *Rumspringa,* some adolescents engage in very rebellious activities, like drinking and smoking and other behavior usually condemned by the Amish community. The grace part is young people are not bound by our laws because they have not taken membership in the church, so we overlook the wild behavior."

Gary nodded. "So anyway, something happened to Stephen that frightened him badly. He wouldn't tell his mother what it was. He came home one night, and she said he was terrified. Steven packed his bag, left that night, and the next day he joined the army. He never came home again until he returned from Vietnam, after he received a head wound fighting in the Tet offensive. The wound and his experiences in Southeast Asia gave him post-traumatic stress syndrome. When he came home, his mother said he could remember nothing of his life before the army. Steven spent many years in different VA hospitals and then could finally come home. He moved out to the farm where we found him. He survived on his army pension, disability payments and Social Security. He also did odd jobs for people. Mostly he kept to himself and remained pretty low key."

Jenny nodded. "And his mother does not know what happened to him that drove him out of town?"

"None whatsoever. She said the night he left, he just rushed in, packed his bags and took off. He said hardly a word, but she could tell he was horrified by something. She has told us over and over that Stephen came home from Vietnam very troubled by all the killing he saw and that he swore to her he would never kill again. She says he has never lied to her."

Jenny's eyes brightened. "Okay. Now tell me about the women that were killed."

Elbert took out a notebook and flipped through some pages. "Anna Myerson, Liz Ingersoll, and Missy Berringer. Anna Myerson, twenty years old, lived in Wooster and attended Wooster College. Wooster is a liberal arts school and, to my way of thinking, kind of airy-fairy. Myerson was an outstanding student though, well-liked and studying for a degree in biology. She was a beautiful girl, and her friends said she wanted to teach at the high school level. Quiet, no police record, a stay-at-home-and-study-hard kind of girl. She was an avid hiker and biker and often visited the parks and trails around Wooster. Her favorites seemed to be Grosjean Park and Wooster Park and we think Lambright knew her routine and followed her there on the day she was killed."

Jenny shook her head. "Except that until proven guilty, you don't know that it was Stephen Lambright who killed her."

Elbert smiled. "You're right. Let me rephrase that. We think the killer knew her routine."

"And the other women?"

"Liz Ingersoll was fifty-two and worked at the Buckle My Shoe Preschool on Chase Street. She was born in Wayne County but left in her teen years. She had just recently returned to town and gone to work at the school. She also was quiet, single, kept to herself, and loved children. The people at the school said she was one of the best aides they ever had."

"And Missy Berringer?"

"Twenty-two, lived in Wooster, worked as a barmaid at Midge's Fool's Paradise in Craigton. It's an upscale singles bar and has a constant turnover of clientele. Lots of people in and out. Missy was beautiful, popular with the customers, made a lot of money in tips and lived in Wooster."

"Boyfriend or husband?"

"No, currently uninvolved. Her boss said she had recently broken off with her boyfriend, though."

"Did anyone follow up on the boyfriend?"

The two policemen looked at each other. "Well, we caught up with Lambright so quickly and everything seemed to fall into place, we just..."

Jenny smiled. "Put all your eggs in one basket?"

Gary could feel his face reddening. "Yes, ma'am, we kind of did that."

Jenny got a serious look. "What do we know about murder, Detective?"

"In what way?"

"Most murders are committed for one of several reasons: love, sex and jealousy, to hide a secret, greed, revenge, obsession and hate, money, psychosis and mental disorders, or getting or keeping power. There are others, but they don't seem to fit here. With our victims, there are interesting circumstances that probably should have been investigated. Anna Myerson, a beautiful athletic girl that might have caught the attention of a sexual predator. Liz Ingersoll, another person who left town in their teens, like Stephen Lambright. And Missy Berringer, who recently split up with her boyfriend."

Elbert looked at Jenny. "Where are you going with this?"

"It feels to me like the solution to this case fell into place too easily. If it were up to me, I would do a little more looking around."

Elbert nodded. "Well, it would help to have you ask a few questions among the Amish... wherever that leads you. I certainly wouldn't want to railroad an innocent man."

"But, Lieutenant," Gary said, "we have all the evidence we need."

"Well, it is mostly circumstantial evidence, Detective." He looked at Jenny. "One thing I've learned in the last few years is if this lady makes a suggestion, we should probably follow it."

He turned back to Jenny. "When will Bobby be here?"

"It's Monday, and he's due on Thursday."

"I can offer you the same arrangement we have had before. Interested?"

"I think so, Elbert. I'll talk to Bobby when he gets here. More cake?"

# NEW INQUIRIES

Bobby Halverson shook his head. "You have always been impulsive, my dear Jenny. I've done a little research on this case and Elbert has wrapped it up pretty tight."

Jenny shook her head. "I know, Uncle Bobby, but I have a feeling that something isn't right. Or there is something that has been hidden for a long time and needs to be brought to light."

"What makes you think that?"

"Well, looking back at our other cases, it felt like I got nudges in my heart to go in a certain direction. When we solved the quilt case, it was finding my mama's signature heart on the quilt wrapped around Emma Johnson that helped us solve it, like a message from the past. And then when we followed the Danny Wittmer case, I found those old pictures of Jonathan. He was a hippy back then and yet the real Jonathan was hidden inside. I kept hearing the phrase 'Nothing is as it seems'. And that was exactly how it all worked out. Nothing was as it seemed. Levon Wittmer wasn't Levon Wittmer and Danny wasn't Danny. So, when I heard Stephen Lambright's story, and tied it together with how easily they solved this case, it just didn't feel right."

"Keep going."

"We had to do weeks of legwork to solve the quilt mystery and we traveled to five different states before we found the real Danny Wittmer. And when you look at other serial killers, some took a long time to uncover and the authorities never caught some of them. It just seems like someone made it way too easy for Elbert and Gary to get to Stephen."

Bobby nodded. "That is something to think about. They never caught the Zodiac out in San Francisco. And it took years to find the Green River Killer in Seattle."

"Yes, and I wonder why I found that letter from my papa hidden in my desk all those years. I've sat at that desk hundreds of times without ever knowing that just a few inches away was something precious. It reminds me of the story of Mr. Worthington's stamps."

"Mr. Worthington's stamps?"

"Yes, Mr. Worthington was a very wealthy man in Wooster. He was ill for quite some time and then died and left 'everything' to a niece and nephew. But when they examined his bank accounts, the 'everything' turned out to be practically nothing at all. His relatives were counting on the money and it was a great disappointment. They remembered Mr. Worthington had always said the safest way to keep your money was to buy gold bullion and bury it, so his niece and nephew believed he had purchased gold and hidden it somewhere on the property. They searched for several weeks and dug up almost every inch of the lawn, but they soon reached the point where they were thinking they might have to sell the house because they had no money to keep it up. In the process of all this, they found that their uncle had sold securities and drawn out enormous sums of money from his accounts, but they did not know what he had done with the proceeds."

"A genuine dilemma."

"Yes. I got involved because a friend of theirs asked me to help them by using my brain to figure out an obvious place where old Mr. Worthington might have hidden the money. I went over to the house and, after looking around, I suggested perhaps there might be a secret drawer in the desk, something like what Papa did to my desk. I was thinking he left a treasure map or something of that sort. Well, there wasn't a secret drawer, at least not one we could find, and all they found in the desk were some old love letters from a girl in Indiana. I looked at them and it all became clear. I asked the niece to show me a copy of her uncle's signature and sure enough, it was very plain that the uncle had sent them to himself from a fictitious person."

Bobby's brow furrowed. "So, the uncle sent himself love letters? Why would he do that?"

Jenny laughed. "He did it so that he could leave something lying around in plain sight no one would even look at."

"What does that have to do with it?"

"Don't you see, Bobby? The fortune was on the letters. Mr. Worthington had collected four of the most valuable stamps in the world and stuck them on the letters. They were worth millions."

"So, the money was right in front of their eyes and they never saw it."

"Yes! And the scary thing was that the nephew was going to clean out the desk and throw all the 'junk' away. He was very appreciative, I must say."

Bobby leaned back in his chair. "Jenny Hershberger, you

never cease to amaze and amuse me. So, I guess this means that we should start looking for something that's right in front of our faces."

"Yes. And I also think it has to do with Steven Lambright's past. That letter from my papa got me thinking about that. So, let's do some digging. I think we start with the dead girls."

---

THE NEXT DAY, JENNY AND BOBBY PULLED UP IN FRONT OF A duplex in a quiet section of Wooster. They went to the door of Apartment 206. Jenny knocked and in a minute the door opened and a pretty, young blonde girl looked out. "Sheriff Halverson?"

Bobby nodded. "Yes. We called this morning. It's very good of you to see us so soon. This is Jenny Hershberger. She and I work together as special investigators for the Wooster Police Department."

"An Amish woman working for the police?"

Jenny smiled. "I know it seems odd, but the crimes we have worked on involved the Amish community, as does the Stephen Lambright case. All will be made clear, uh,..."

"Oh, excuse me. I'm Diana Woodward. Please come in, and yes, this is a good day because the three of us... I mean, the two of us don't have classes today."

The young lady put a handkerchief to her eyes and wiped them. "I'm sorry. I'm still very upset about all this. We were so close. And Anna had her whole life in front of her." Jenny stepped forward and put an arm around Diana's shoulder. "It's all right, dear. We understand. If you want us to come back another time..."

"No, no. Do come in. It's fine. I'll be all right. Just talking to you will probably help us."

Diana ushered them inside. Another girl was sitting on the couch. She was a redhead and also very pretty. Diana went and sat next to her on the couch. "This is Madison Jenkins. Madison and Anna and I, well, our friends called us the three musketeers. Madison, this is Jenny Hershberger and Sheriff Halverson."

Bobby smiled. "Retired."

Madison put out her hand, and Jenny and Bobby shook it. She looked at Jenny. "So, how can we help you? The police have already been here, of course, but they didn't stay long."

"Just long enough to verify Anna's ID and her address," Diana said. "We never really got to tell anyone about Anna."

Jenny sat down in a chair across from the girls and Bobby pulled a chair from the kitchen dinette. Jenny smiled at the girls. "Then why don't you tell us about Anna? Take all the time you want. Even little things."

Diana looked puzzled. "If the police are so sure that Steven Lambright killed Anna, then why exactly are you here?"

Bobby looked over at Jenny. "Jenny... Mrs. Hershberger... has a real knack for getting to the truth. She was instrumental in solving the Emma Johnson case and the Danny Wittmer case. And she does a lot of her work based on intuition and her innate knowledge of what makes people tick—why they do the things they do. Something about this case and the rapidity of the arrest of Stephen Lambright just didn't seem right to Jenny. And when we talked it over, I agreed. We took our concerns to Lieutenant Wainwright at the police department and, since we have worked with Lieutenant Wainwright before, he asked us to follow up on some details the police may have overlooked. To avoid a rush to judgment."

"Oh, I see."

Jenny leaned forward in her chair. "So, tell us all about Anna. There may be something in what we learn the police may have missed."

"Do you think that Stephen Lambright did not kill Anna?"

Jenny shook her head. "I'm not saying that... yet. It's just a feeling I have that there is something hidden in this case that may surprise us all."

Jenny noticed a strange look on Madison's face, but Diana went on.

"Anna was born and raised in California. She was a fitness fanatic. She ate organic food and had a gluten-free diet and did a lot of biking and running. She was buff. She got us both into it."

"Did Anna have a boyfriend?"

Diana looked away. "Anna was way too focused on finishing her education and getting her career going. Oh, she had plenty of boys that desperately wanted to go out with her. But she just didn't have the time. She came from a very successful family in San Diego and was determined to make good and show her parents she wasn't just a California Barbie Doll. She said there would be plenty of time for romance later. But she never..." Diana wiped her eyes again. "Oh, it's just so terrible. Why would anyone want to hurt Anna?"

"So, she really didn't go out much?"

"Only to exercise or run. The rest of the time she was slamming the books. And it paid off. She was getting straight A's. She had a bright future ahead of her. And now..."

"I've had that feeling too." Jenny looked over at Madison. The quiet girl had a set to her chin.

"What do you mean, Madison?"

"The feeling you talked about, like there is something more than what the police think. On the day she died, before she left for the park, Anna told me that someone was watching her. She saw him when she went to the springs."

"And did she tell you more?"

"She said that this man was in the parking lot at Grosvenor Park two or three times when she came back from the springs. He was in a white van, just sitting. She heard some music, so she figured he was just enjoying the park, like she was. Then the last time she was there, she saw him looking at her and it made her feel weird, fearful, she said."

Bobby spoke up. "Did she describe the man?"

Madison nodded. "She said he had on sunglasses and was wearing a floppy hat that hid his face."

"And she said he was in a white van?"

"Yes, she did. And she took down the license number."

"Do you have it?"

Madison stood up and went into another room. She returned with her purse. "She wrote it down. Like I said, she was a detail freak."

Madison handed Jenny a slip of paper. RYB 9194.

"That's Steven Lambright's license plate. Did she tell you anything else about him?"

Madison furrowed her brow. "This is the strange part. Steven Lambright has long stringy hair and is unshaven. Anna said this man had a mustache and she was almost positive he had a trimmed beard. I don't think Steven Lambright could have grown long hair in two weeks."

"So, you are sure about this?"

Madison nodded. "Anna noticed everything. She was

going to be a biologist, so she practiced observing everything around her. It was a little foible of hers. If she was pretty sure the man had a mustache and a trimmed beard, he probably did."

---

JENNY AND BOBBY CLIMBED INTO BOBBY'S TRUCK. JENNY WAS thoughtful.

Bobby started the engine. "So, Jenny, what are you thinking.?"

"Well, two things. I'm thinking that we now have a monkey wrench in the works—another man who may not be Steven Lambright driving Steven's white van. Of course, he could have had his hair tucked up under the hat. But it certainly raises some red flags."

"And what is the second thing?"

"I'm thinking we should go over to *Der Dutchman* Restaurant and get some pork chops, followed by cherry pie with ice cream."

Bobby nodded his head vigorously. "Great minds think alike, my dear. Great minds think alike."

# MISSY

obby pulled up to Midge's Fool's Paradise in Craigton. It was early in the evening, not yet five o'clock, but the place was already jumping. Bobby was on his own. Jenny had taken a pass on visiting the singles bar. She smiled and shook her head when Bobby asked her. "My elders are pretty understanding, Bobby, but I think going to Midge's would definitely cross a line. Drop me by the library and I'll follow up on Liz Ingersoll instead."

So, Bobby was 'baching' it. He walked into the club. It was very upscale, nothing sleazy about it at all. The décor was top drawer, and the crowd was energetic but classy. Well-dressed women sat with older men at the bar or at tables. Younger women and men served the patrons a variety of cocktails. Bobby did not see any bottled beer at all on the trays, but he saw some drafts in fancy glasses. He walked up to the lady at the reception and asked to see the owner. After showing his I.D. as a special investigator for Elbert Wainwright, the girl escorted him to a very plush office in the back of the building. An older, well-dressed woman greeted him and ushered him in. She waved him to a well-stuffed chair and then arranged herself on a very nice couch across from him.

"Midge Payton?"

She smiled. "Yes, and you are Sheriff Bobby Halverson."

"Retired."

"But still doing police work, Sheriff?"

Bobby nodded. "I'm kind of like the old fire horse who sticks up his ears, snorts and races around the pasture when the fire trucks go by."

Midge smiled. "I hardly think so, Sheriff. I grew up in Wayne Country and I remember your term as sheriff very well. I was in high school then, and as I recollect, we were pretty well-behaved, given that the alternative was a tongue-lashing or worse by the sheriff."

"Oh, I don't think I was all that fearsome, Mrs. Payton."

"Miss Payton, Sheriff. I never married." She gestured at the surrounding room. "This is what I'm married to. And it provides for me better than any husband I could think of." She took Bobby's still stalwart figure in with a quick glance and ginned coyly. "Now, if you were just a few years younger..."

Bobby shook his head and grinned. "Jenny warned me that this place might be dangerous."

They both laughed. "So, Sheriff Halverson, how can I help you? I assume you want to talk about Missy Berringer?"

"Yes, Miss Payton..."

"Please, call me Midge." She saw Bobby glance around uncomfortably. "It's all right, Sheriff, just to make this mess a bit less formal, if that's okay."

"Sure... Midge. Okay, what can you tell me about Missy Berringer?"

"Too hot for her own good."

"Say again?"

"She thought she was pretty hot stuff, and actually she was. A beautiful girl. I had to call her in and dress her down a few times for being too familiar with the clientele. But she reminded me that most of them were getting too familiar with her. Poor girl. Beauty without brains to back it up. She was always looking for Daddy Warbucks. And her boyfriend didn't like that much. He started some nasty scenes here, and I had to blackball him from the club. A hot head with a real short fuse."

"What's this boyfriend's name?"

"Rod Krieger. We used to call him Hot Rod. About a month ago, Missy had enough of his antics and showed him the door."

"And how did he take that?"

Midge shook her head. "Not well. Not well at all. He busted in here the night she dumped him and threatened Missy in front of about ten of my customers."

Bobby was interested. "What did he say?"

"He said he was going to kill her. It was like one of those movies where the guy says 'If I can't have you, nobody will.' I had to get my biggest guys to toss him. And before that there were the times that Missy came to work with lots of makeup covering a black eye he gave her."

"And where does this Hot Rod live?"

"Dalton. When Missy ordered him out of her place, he moved into an apartment over there with a couple of his low-life buddies. I think his problem is cocaine. He probably smokes it. Nobody is that ready to flare up unless they are amped to the gills."

Midge noted the surprise on Bobby's face when she used an expression from the drug world. She smiled. "Listen, Sheriff. I have been around the quad a couple of times. I get all kinds in here. Folks that you would think are totally respectable, but they live on the dark side most of the time. I try to keep the riff-raff out of my place, you know, but I have a living to make, too."

Bobby nodded slowly. "Listen, Midge. When you were on the east side of the quad, I was probably over on the west. When you are a sheriff, you see it all. Nothing surprises me, so don't worry. What you say to me here stays here." He pulled out a notebook. "You got an address for Rod-boy?"

"The Fenimore Apartments in Dalton."

"In Westerville Park?"

"That's the place."

"Pretty tony apartments for a club hanger."

"Oh, didn't I tell you? Rod is the son of a very well-to-do real estate developer in Wooster. Ben Krieger. That's why Missy hooked up with him. She saw a chance to punch her ticket. But sometimes the ticket costs too much. Rod was just a psycho."

Bobby stood up. "I guess I'll go make a call on our friend, Rod Krieger."

Midge's brow furrowed. "Sheriff, I know you are probably in pretty good shape..."

Bobby grinned. "For an old guy?"

"Well, I wasn't going to say it." She smiled. "I was just going to suggest that you take a couple of husky young streets with you. Rod is pretty volatile, and if he's hopped up he could be dangerous."

"Thanks, Midge. I'll take your advice. And don't get up. I'll find my way out."

Bobby turned to go.

"Sheriff?"

Bobby turned back. "Yes, Midge?"

"Just my humble opinion. I never thought that Lambright killed Missy. I'll put my money on Rod."

"I'll keep that in mind, Midge."

Bobby, Gary Linden, and Bill Cowper sat in an unmarked car across from the Fenimore Apartments. Bill Cowper pulled out a pad. "He lives in Apartment 12, second floor in the back."

Gary looked over at Bobby. "We have uniforms, and we also have a warrant to search the apartment for drugs. He lives with known drug dealers and we've been helping the Dalton boys try to clean up this part of Wayne County. So, your timing couldn't be better."

"Timing is everything in the Kingdom."

"Say what?"

Bobby smiled. "Just something the pastor at my church in Paradise used to say. If you boys don't mind, I think I'll just sit here and spectate. I'm sure you have it covered."

"I was going to suggest that, anyway." He nodded to Bill. "Everything in place?"

Bill clicked the switch on a walkie-talkie. "Status report."

The unit crackled and then voices came on. "Team one in place..." another crackle. "Team two set."

"Okay, boys, let's go get them."

Gary and Bill climbed out of the car and headed across the street. Bobby pulled out a Camel and lit up. He grinned to himself.

*Better them than me!*

Rod Krieger glared across the table at Gary and Bill. Bobby leaned his chair back against the wall behind them. Krieger was flushed and sweating. "What's the deal here? You guys have no reason to haul me in."

"Actually, Rod, we have about one hundred grams worth of reasons to haul you in. My dad used to tell me that if you want to be a winner, don't hang out with losers. Your roommates are real losers. We are focused on cleaning up Wayne County and so when you throw a big net, all the fish get caught. We had a search warrant for your apartment and... bingo... the stash of the week in the hall closet. What about that?"

"I know nothing about that stuff. I was just renting a room."

"So, if we took a blood test, we wouldn't find cocaine in your system?"

Rod's head jerked, and his eyes went from face to face. He looked trapped. "Yeah, okay, I might have had a toot or two."

Gary locked his hands together and flexed his knuckles. "Well, I don't think you're just an innocent dilettante. We believe you free-base, and regularly. You're in a big pickle here, Rod. You and your buddies all live there. We watch a lot of activity in and out of the place and then we find one hundred grams of extremely pure cocaine in the closet. How are we to know that you're not in on it?" Gary glanced at Bobby.

Bobby took over. "Unless, of course, you can give us some details about the operation. Like the name of the big supplier in this region and some other information."

"Who's this guy?"

Gary looked at Bobby. "This is former Sheriff Bobby Halverson. He's a special investigator for us now and, as I recall, when he was sheriff, there was not a lot of drug activity in Wayne County. Not a man to be messed with."

"If I give you the name of the head honcho, they'll kill me."

"If you don't, you'll go to prison for a long time for that and other crimes."

"Yeah, what crimes?"

Bobby stood up and walked to the table. "The murder of Missy Berringer, for one."

"Missy! Aww, you're nuts. I didn't kill Missy. That Lambright nut job did it."

"Well, that's what everyone thought, but some information has come to us that puts the entire case on shaky ground. And if Lambright didn't do it, there is another very conspicuous subject, and that's you."

"I don't know what you are talking about."

Bobby shook his head. "It's about time you stopped with the tough guy attitude and started working with us. We have at least ten witnesses who were there when you walked into Midge's and threatened to kill Missy. And we have others who will testify that you slapped her around from time to time. A proper gentleman."

To their surprise, Rod put his head down on the table and started sobbing. The three men glanced at each other. It was uncomfortable. Finally, Rod spoke. "Why would I kill Missy? She was the only girl I ever loved. I just couldn't get a handle on the coke and it made me wild. I would see her flirting with those old men, and it drove me crazy. She told me she was just playing the angles, getting them to tip her big, but I didn't believe her. So, I kept slapping her around when I saw her doing it. Finally, she had enough. But, before she threw me out, she told me that if I went to rehab and cleaned up, she might consider taking me back, that she did really love me. I was going to do it, go to rehab, straighten out. But when that guy killed her, my life just fell down the well. I had nothing to live for, so I just took up with those guys and tried to kill myself with drugs. I swear, I swear... I didn't kill her." He put his head back down. "Missy... Missy..."

After the guard took Rod back to his cell, Bobby looked at Gary and Bill. "I don't know about this guy. He's got every marker to be the killer... jilted lover, coke freak, hair trigger temper. The crying seemed genuine, but it could have been an act. He might just be a spoiled little rich kid who got in over his head, or he could be a cold-blooded killer. But you should let him cold-turkey his habit for a few days and then we'll see if his answers are a little less emotional. Anyway, you're going to have him in county jail for quite a spell so he's not going anywhere."

Gary and Bill agreed, and Bobby headed back to the Springer house.

13

LIZ

Jenny walked into the Wayne County Library in downtown Wooster. A flood of memories rushed at her, like a sleeper wave. There was the doorway where she had peeked out, watching Jonathan Hershberger circle the block, looking for her after their first tempestuous meeting in the street out front.

*He almost ran me over. I was thinking about finding my birth mother and didn't pay attention to the light.*

Jenny giggled.

*Then he ran his hippie van up on the curb and bent the axle. He was so angry. And his clothes! Oh my.*

She giggled again. A lady coming through the front door looked at her curiously as she passed. Jenny turned and walked through the inner doors.

*So many memories. I found out the entire history of my family here, all the way back to the 1500s in Poland.*

Across the library, the small glassed-in meeting room that used to be her "office" was unoccupied, but now there was a computer on the desk. She walked up to the reception area. The woman who passed her in the foyer was now busy behind the counter, arranging some books and a display of flyers about local events. Another woman who had been working there came out of a door to the left marked "Private." She had her coat on and was carrying her purse.

"Goodnight, Alma. See you tomorrow."

The woman behind the counter waved. She was older, probably about Jenny's age. Jenny stepped up.

The woman looked at her again. "Can I help you?"

Jenny glanced over at the little meeting room. "I was wondering if I could work in that room for a while. I need to do some genealogical research. And do you still have the Biography and Genealogy Master Index?"

The woman smiled. "Yes, you may use that room and yes, we still have the Index, but it's all on that computer on the desk. If you are unfamiliar, I'll show you how to use it."

"That would be most kind."

The two women walked over to the room. Alma unlocked the door and Jenny stepped inside. Jenny looked at the chair in front of the desk.

*That's where Jonathan sat when I showed him that his family had Amish roots and that he and I were very distant cousins... by adoption, of course.*

A tear came to Jenny's eye. She quickly brushed it away.

Alma looked at her again, this time searchingly. "Are you all right?"

Jenny nodded. "Yes. Just a memory, a lovely one. I used to work in this room a lot when I was a teenager. I interned for Mrs. Blake and did a lot of projects for her and..."

A broad smile came over Alma's face. "And your name was Jenny Springer. Of course it was. I thought I knew you. You haven't changed a bit! Do you remember me? I'm Alma Cross, but back then I was Alma Jenkins."

A picture of a skinny, shy young girl with braces came into Jenny's memory. "Why Alma! My goodness, it's been forty years at least?"

Alma nodded. "At least. And you know, I still visit Mrs. Blake. She's living with her daughter and she's a spry ninety-two years old. Wait until I tell her I saw Jenny Springer."

"Mrs. Blake! She was so kind to me. Letting an *etwas verrückt* Amish girl help her. I learned so much from her. And I've been Jenny Hershberger almost since the last time I saw you."

Alma turned on the computer. "Of course. Jenny Hershberger, who's become Ohio's most famous detective. You know, I read about how you helped solve those two cases for Detective Wainwright. Well, he's a lieutenant now... Anyway, that was so interesting to me. I guess it's because anybody who works in a library has a little detective in them. Oh, and I read your book about the Polish Princess who was the ancestor of your family. It was so intriguing. I've been trying to write some of my family history..." Alma paused, then grinned. "Oh, you have things to do and here I am cackling away like a magpie. Let me show you how to use this."

She clicked an icon on the desktop and an application opened on the screen. "Instead of looking in the index at the back of the book, all you have to do is enter the name of the person you are looking for in this little search window."

She put in a name, clicked the search icon, and after a second, a list of family names and relatives appeared. Jenny nodded. "Boy, that will make this a cinch. Thank you, Alma. Will you be here until the library closes, in case I need to ask you some questions?"

"We close at 9:00 and I'm the graveyard shift, so I will be here until then. Do you need any note paper?"

Jenny shook her head. "I brought a notebook and pencils, thank you."

"If you need to print anything out, just pull down this menu. See where it says 'print'? That will print out the whole page. It prints at the front desk, so just come collect it."

"Great! Thanks again."

Jenny slipped into the comfortable desk chair and spent a moment familiarizing herself with the program. There was a search window with four blank fields below it. In the field marked "First Names" she entered Liz, then Ingersoll in the next, Wooster, Ohio as the place lived and from what she had read on the police report she entered 1950 as the birth date. In a few seconds, a new page opened titled, "Historical records found for Liz Ingersoll."

Several sections filled the screen with different people and a slew of family relationships. There were also residences listed and towns where the different people were born. Altogether, it was confusing, but Jenny plugged away. At the end of two hours and a lot of dead ends, Jenny was ready to call it quits. There was a knock on the glass door. Alma was standing there and Jenny waved her in.

"Any luck, Jenny?"

Jenny frowned and shook her head. "No, not yet. I'm about to call it a day."

"Is this something to do with those 3 X 3 murders?"

Jenny looked up. "Yes, how did you know?"

Alma shrugged. "Like I said, if you work in a library, you've got to have a little detective in you. You came back to Apple Creek two years ago to help Lieutenant Wainwright with the girl in the box murder, and then you came last year and found Danny Wittmer alive right here in the hospital. Now here you are again and I figure it has to be connected with this latest case. Gosh Jenny, you're like the Amish Miss

Marple. So, I put two and two together, or should I say three and three together and..."

Jenny smiled. "Very perceptive, Alma. Yes, I'm trying to get some background on one of the murdered women, but I just can't seem to find anything about her."

"Which one are you searching for?"

"Liz Ingersoll."

"Oh, Liz. Well, no wonder you can't find her. Ingersoll was the name of her second husband."

"You knew her?"

"Oh, sure. After she moved back to town, Liz used to come in here all the time before she died. She worked at the Buckle My Shoe Pre-school and she was always looking for new books to read at story hour. Loved kids. I do too, so we struck up a friendship, and she told me some of her story over coffee. She grew up around here but left when she was eighteen. She got into some kind of trouble—she never told me what—and left town in a hurry. She went to Indiana and met a man there. They were married and lived in Indiana for a few years, but her husband, who was a druggie and an alcoholic, died. An overdose, she said. Then she moved out west and married a guy named Ingersoll, but he left her. So, after forty years she came back home and got a job at the pre-school. Then, after all that, she gets murdered. Sad."

"Murder is always sad. Did Liz tell you her maiden name?"

"Yes, she told me. It was Gingerich."

"Gingerich? But that's an Amish name."

"Amish? She didn't mention that."

"Wait a minute. Let me search for her again."

Jenny put in Elizabeth Gingerich, Wooster, Ohio and birth date in 1950. A whole new set of information came up.

Elizabeth Gingerich, born in Sugar Creek Township, Wayne County Ohio. She stared at the information in amazement.

*Sugar Creek Township is right near where my mama got lost in the big snowstorm in 1950. It's only five miles from Apple Creek! Oh, my goodness. Liz Ingersoll was Amish. Look at her relatives: Richert, Gingerich, Steiner, Kirchofer, Schlabach...*

Jenny looked up from the screen. "Oh, Alma, you are a God-send. This is amazing. She was Amish."

---

Bobby and Jenny sat together at the kitchen table the next morning, enjoying some hot *Kaffee*. Bobby put down his cup.

"So, one of our gals is Amish. That's interesting. Lambright is Amish, too. And they both left the church and then left town when they were young. Something happened that scared them and they both jumped ship. Lambright just up and joins the army, and he's off to Vietnam and Liz Ingersoll runs away and stays missing for forty years. Something happened, something neither one could handle, and I'm betting that it happened at the same time to both of them. I think we need to dig into this and find out what's up. Seems like there's a connection between Lambright and Liz. A connection that implies more than just a random killing."

Jenny nodded. "I know there is Bobby. Sugar Creek is just a quarter mile down Kidron Road from where Henry Lowenstein ran off the road in the snowstorm back in 1950... the day before my mama found me at Jepson's pond. And every case we've worked on with Elbert has some connection to my past. I'm beginning to understand that the past holds the key to this case. Something from the past is the common denominator in this. It is so strange that I was at a dead end trying to find Liz in the genealogy records until Alma came over and told me her maiden name. And Alma knew her from a casual meeting at the Library? What are the odds? I think the Lord is showing me something here." Jenny pulled out a notebook. "Liz Ingersoll's parents were Walter and Wanda Gingerich. Her Grandparents were Ruth and Roy Kirchofer. We need to see if we can track them down."

Bobby nodded an affirmative and then added a thought. "I think it would be a good idea if we talked to Steven Lambright's mother first. We need to find out what happened to Steven before he left town. It was obviously something that shook him badly and I would like to hear it unfiltered from Steven's mother."

"That's a good idea." Jenny looked at the wall clock. "We have plenty of time to make some calls. I'll fix some bacon and eggs and then we will go."

---

SAMANTHA LAMBRIGHT LIFTED THE CHINA POT FROM THE small coffee table in front of her couch. "More *kaffee?*

Jenny put her hand over her cup and smiled. "Not for me, Mrs. Lambright." Bobby just nodded, and Samantha filled his cup.

"Now, how can I help you, Jenny? Before you answer, I must tell you how grateful I am that you have gotten involved in this *kerfuffle.* I feel as though *der leiber Gott* has answered my prayers. Now... ask me anything."

"We want to know about the time that Steven abruptly left home and joined the army. Lieutenant Wainwright told us a little, but we would like to hear the complete story from you."

Samantha put the *Kaffee* down and folded her hands on

her lap. "Steven was a good boy. He loved being Amish. He helped his father on the farm from the time he was little. And then Mervin was killed working in the fields, a terrible accident. Steven was fourteen and he was working with Mervin in the wheat harvest and he got distracted. He walked into the path of the reaping machine and Mervin jumped in between to shove him out of the way. He saved Steven, but the reaper ran over Mervin and killed him. Steven was never the same after that." She paused and wiped her eyes with a hanky. "Steven blamed himself for his father's death. He became a loner, very secretive about every-thing he did. He would disappear for hours at a time. He dropped out of school and stayed out in the woods or wandering in the hills. I think he met someone during this time, someone that he spent a lot of time with, but he never told me who it was. This went on for the next three years. Then one night... it was very late. Steven came home in a rush. He was terrified. He kept looking out the window. Then he ran upstairs, packed some clothing in a suitcase, and ran back down. 'I have to get out of here, Mama, he said.' I begged him to tell me what happened, but he wouldn't. He didn't even stay the night. When I asked him where he was going, he said he would be in touch. Then he left. I didn't hear from him for two months. Then I got a letter from Oklahoma. Steven had joined the army and gone to Fort Sill for basic training. He was leaving for Vietnam. That's all he said. I didn't see him or hear from him for two years. Then he was injured severely during the Tet Offensive. Because I was listed as the nearest of kin, they sent him to the VA Central Ohio Health Care clinic in Columbus. I went to see him, but he had a hard time remembering who I was. He was wounded in the head during the battle and he lost all memory of his childhood... anything before the war. He remembered one thing—that Jesus said it was wrong to kill. He swore to me he would never kill again. When the army decided he had recovered enough to go active again, he ran away. They were going to put him in prison, but a kind doctor convinced them to put him in long-term care. He was there off and on for almost twenty-five years. When he got out, he was just a shell of the boy I raised here in Ohio."

"When did this all happen, Samantha?"

"The summer of 1967… July 5. I remember because it was right after the holiday. "

Jenny took a deep breath and looked at Bobby. "That's an amazing story, Samantha. Did you know that Liz Ingersoll was born Elizabeth Gingerich and that her family was Amish also?"

Samantha's eyes widened. "*Wirklich? Das ist erstaunlich.*"

"Yes, it is amazing, and I think it has a lot to do with this entire case. We are going to visit Liz's parents—they only live a few miles from here."

"That's odd. I never met them. But they could be in a different group. Sometimes I think the Amish are like all the mainline churches—so many denominations that don't speak to each other."

Jenny and Bobby got up to leave.

"Please keep me informed, Jenny. I want to know everything. And I will be praying."

"Thank you, Samantha. I have a feeling we will need it."

14

## WHAT HAPPENED?

The old farm, unlike most Amish farms, appeared run down and decrepit. The barn roof was sagging in the middle and the paint had peeled off the house long ago. Bobby drove his truck up a dirt track that turned off Ashland Road. The driveway, pitted and full of potholes, kept the truck bouncing crazily. It was almost as if the owners didn't want anyone coming to visit them. Bobby eased the truck to a stop in front of the house. The drawn blinds covered the windows and dead grass poked up through cracks in the sidewalk leading up to the porch. The weather had changed and an icy wind rustled what remained of the leaves hanging in the Buckeyes that closed in around the house. As they got out of the car, a raven croaked mournfully in the top of a tree.

Jenny shivered and pulled her sweater closer around her. "Feels like winter's coming, Bobby."

"Another one? Seems like we just had one."

They walked up the steps to the front porch. The house seemed about to collapse. It was so uncared for. A swing hung by one chain at the end of the porch, the other end sitting on the wooden deck. It swung fitfully in a half-circle, back and forth, as the wind plucked at it. Jenny opened the screen door and knocked on the yellow glass door window. Nothing. She knocked again.

Bobby walked to the end of the porch and looked around the corner into the side yard.

"Doesn't look like anyone is here. Let's go."

They turned and started down the steps and as they did, out of the corner of her eye, Jenny caught sight of a movement behind the window curtains. "Wait, Bobby."

They stopped. Jenny slowly turned her head, just in time to see the curtain close. "There's someone in there, Bobby. I saw the curtain move. Let's try again."

Jenny turned back to the door. "Hello, we are here to just ask a few questions about Elizabeth Gingerich. We don't want to cause any problems. I know you are in there because I saw the curtain move. We just wonder if you wouldn't mind talking to us."

They waited for a minute, and then they heard the dead bolt on the front door snap back. The door opened just a crack, and a voice said quietly, "Okay, go ahead. If you get out of line, I'll lock the door and that would be the time for you to leave. What do you want to know?"

"First, I'm Jenny Hershberger. I grew up in Apple Creek, and this is Sheriff Bobby Halverson, retired."

"I know who you are. What do you want?"

"We want to know if you are related to the woman known as Liz Ingersoll?"

"The one who was killed?"

"Yes. She used to be my daughter."

"So, you are Wanda Gingerich?"

"Yes, how did you find me?"

Jenny stepped closer. "Mrs. Gingerich, would you mind if we came in? It's very difficult to speak to you through the door and Sheriff Halverson and I think we can help put this case to rest if we can just get a few answers. And it is nippy out here."

"Steven Lambright killed her—that's all that needs to be said."

Bobby looked at Jenny and nodded for her to go on.

"That's just it, Mrs. Gingerich. We don't really believe that Mr. Lambright killed your daughter."

"What do you mean?" The woman behind the door opened it just a crack.

"We think that something happened to both your daughter and Steven Lambright years ago, something that is behind all of this, and we want to find out what it was and see if we can't set it right. There are just too many coincidences."

"What do you care whether Elizabeth died or if Steven Lambright gets a lethal injection for it?"

"Please, Mrs. Gingerich. We only want a few minutes of your time. Can't we come in?"

There was a moment of silence and the door slowly opened. "All right, come in. You've got my interest. I want to hear what you have to say."

The woman stepped back and motioned for Jenny and Bobby to come in. They both stepped in and she closed the door. Then she turned and started down the hall. She led them into a dark room off the main hallway. A single flickering kerosene lamp stood on a small table by a couch. The atmosphere was dank and stuffy. Mrs. Gingerich motioned for them to sit on the couch and she sat in an old stuffed chair across from them and looked at them with a peculiar gaze.

"So, what do you mean, something happened?"

Bobby started. "What we know, after talking to Mr. Lambright's mother, is this: Steven Lambright's father was killed in an accident when Steven was fourteen and it affected Steven deeply. His mother says he changed completely. He became very secretive, and she believes he met someone who befriended him. Then something terrible happened, something that terrified him and made him run away. He joined the army and went to Vietnam. That was the summer of 1967."

Jenny spoke up. "Then just last night I learned that something happened to Liz...Elizabeth... around the same time that made her run away, too. So, what I want to ask is, what was it that happened to Liz and when did it happen?"

Mrs. Gingerich had a puzzled look on her face. "You say it happened in 1967? In the summer? Yes, that was when Elizabeth ran away."

Jenny leaned forward. "Do you remember the exact time, Mrs. Gingerich?"

"It was right around the fourth of July in 1967."

Jenny looked at Bobby. "See, Bobby? I knew it. Something happened that scared Steven and something also scared Elizabeth at exactly the same time. And my sense tells me those two things are the same." She turned back to Mrs. Gingerich. "Do you have any idea what happened?"

The woman shook her head. "I don't have the vaguest notion."

Bobby leaned in. "Perhaps her father knows..."

Mrs. Gingerich's eyes narrowed. "Him? He's dead. And the world is a better place for it."

There was silence. Then Bobby spoke. "Do you care to expound on that, Mrs. Gingerich?"

She looked up at the ceiling and then around the room.

Finally, she spoke. "I guess it doesn't matter... Lizzie's dead, and he's dead." She sat silent for a moment. "He abused her. You know, physically. He was a pervert. She tried to tell me, but I wouldn't listen. Then I found out it was true. I caught him coming out of her room one night. But I couldn't say anything because he told me he would divorce me if I did, leave me with nothing. So, I kept quiet, looked the other way. Lizzie learned to stay away when he was home. She had a place, you know, where she went. She never told me where it was because... because she didn't trust me. It was somewhere out in the woods. She'd be gone for days. She would come back for food and fresh clothes and sleep when he was in the fields." She put her hands over her face and wept. "Oh, what kind of mother was I? I should have killed him, I should have protected her. But I didn't, and she hated me for it. Then she came home that night. She was terrified, white as a sheet. She went upstairs and filled a suitcase with clothes. She didn't even speak to me, she just left. I never saw her again. I heard she went out to California with Ingersoll, but that was three or four years later. She was in Indiana first. I know because a relative of mine saw her there. She wasn't Amish anymore, and she was living with some of those hippie people. And then about two years ago, her father died and I guess she thought she would be safe back here. But she wasn't... she wasn't."

Jenny and Bobby sat quietly while she sobbed. Finally, Jenny moved over to her and put her arm around her shoulders. They sat that way for a long time.

After a while, Jenny asked one more question. "Mrs. Gingerich, you said that Elizabeth stayed somewhere out in the woods. Do you have any idea where that was?"

The old woman nodded. "There is a big wooded area just across Ashland Road. Wooster Park. The Spangler family donated all that land to the City of Wooster in 1961. They've been upgrading it ever since, but back then it was a wild place. It goes all the way to Highway 302, must be five or six hundred acres. Lots of hills and ravines, trees, brush. A kid could lose herself in there and nobody would find her. If Elizabeth went anywhere to hide, it was in there."

Later, as they were driving home, Jenny spoke up. "So, we have the Gingerich family on one side of Wooster Park and the Lambright farm on the other, over by Highway 302. It doesn't take much to imagine two messed up kids finding each other out in the woods and befriending each other. We need to canvas the area and see if anybody remembers seeing them together out there. I know it's forty years ago, but so was the Emma Johnson murder and we got a lot of help just asking questions."

Bobby grinned. "Okay, but I'd like to get Detective Linden and Sergeant Cowper to do the legwork. I'll drive."

"Bobby, I know there is something from the past that is at the heart of this entire case. And it involves Steven Lambright and Elizabeth Gingerich. Maybe it's time to interview Steven Lambright."

---

ELBERT WAINWRIGHT AND GARY LINDEN SAT WITH BOBBY AND Jenny in the interview room at the Wayne County Jail. They had not been waiting long when the door from the jail section clicked and two guards led Steven Lambright into the room. He was in an orange jail jumpsuit and there were shackles on his hands and feet. His hair was cut shorter, below his ears, but it was still lank and greasy-looking. He was clean-shaven and his jumpsuit was clean, but he shuffled like an old man to the table. The guards motioned for him to sit and he slid into the seat rather than sat. Jenny noticed his eyes were unfocused and that he really did not seem to be present. Elbert started the conversation.

"Steven, I want to introduce you to Jenny Hershberger and Bobby Halverson. They are helping us with this case."

"I didn't kill them... those women. I don't kill people anymore. Jesus was right."

"Hold on a minute, Steven. Jenny is here to help you. She may be the only one, besides your mother, who agrees with you. So, I want you to get present in the room and listen to her. She's here to help."

Steven looked over at the older Amish woman sitting across from him. "You look like my mother."

Jenny smiled. "That's because I am Amish, like your mother, and like you once were."

"I was Amish?"

"A long time ago, Steven. You grew up on an Amish farm. Then you ran away and joined the army."

Steven looked away. "I don't remember that."

Jenny leaned forward. "Do you not remember because you can't, or maybe because there were some terrible things that happened that you don't want to remember?"

Steven reached his shackled hands up to the side of his head and pushed his lank hair back behind his ear. There was a deep furrow starting at his hairline in front and running back to the top left side of his skull.

"See this? That's why they let me wear my hair long. Because of that, I don't remember...anything."

"What caused that, Steven?"

"I don't want to say."

"Please, Steven, it will help me understand."

Steven wiped his eyes with the back of his hands.

Jenny glanced over at Elbert. "Do you think you could

unshackle his hands? Steven won't do anything, will you, Steven?"

Elbert nodded, and the guard stepped forward and unshackled his hands. Steven rubbed his wrists and looked at Jenny with gratitude in his eyes.

"Okay, you're a nice lady. I'll tell you. I was in the army. I was in Vietnam. We were stationed on Highway 1 outside Hué when the North Vietnamese attacked on the 30th of January. The PAVN took over the city. They drove us out. We went back in and had to fight them house-to-house. My buddies were blown to bits all around me. We came down a street and there was a big fifty hidden in a window on the second floor of a building. They cut loose on us and I took a slug right beside my ear. Another bit closer..."

"Thank you, Steven. Now, do you think you could try really hard to remember something from before that?"

Steven paled, but he nodded.

"Do you remember when your father died?"

Steven took a deep breath and his hands shook. "I didn't kill him, I didn't kill him."

"It was an accident, Steven. No one ever blamed you. It was an accident. Please calm yourself."

"Hard, it's hard."

"I know, Steven. Now, just a few more questions. Do you remember Elizabeth?"

A light seemed to come on in Steven's eyes. "Elizabeth? Elizabeth?"

"Yes, your friend, Elizabeth. You stayed in the woods together a long time ago."

"I'm getting tired. I want to sleep. Please don't ask me any more..."

"Just one more, Steven. Have you ever seen this before?"

Jenny reached into her bag and brought out a piece of

white paper. In the middle of it was the signature of the killer... 3 X 3.

Steven Lambright's eyes widened and then he pushed his chair back so hard that he fell over. He scrambled on the floor, trying to get away. "NO! NO! Please, I won't tell. Don't kill me, I won't tell..."

Steven rolled into a fetal position and started screaming. Horrible, piercing screams torn from his very soul.

Elbert shouted to the guard. "Get the doc in here, now!

The rest of them watched in horror as Steven Lambright suffered the tortures of the damned.

# 15

## OLD WOUNDS

*J*enny shook her head as they sat in Elbert's office. "Will he be all right? I did not know that would happen."

Elbert tapped his pencil on the desk, then looked at Jenny. "He has post-traumatic stress disorder and amnesia. They used to call PTSD shell shock back in the day. And for Steven, that's what it is. The horrible things that happened in battle caused real shock to his system. Then the wound to his head injured his brain and caused what the doctors call retrograde amnesia—the type of amnesia which causes a person to forget events that occurred prior to their injury." He looked at a note on his desk. "Some symptoms are memory loss, confusion and disorientation, agitation and distress and aggressive behaviors."

"But, Elbert, he remembered something from before the injury, something tied into the 3 X 3 killings. That signature terrified him. So maybe his brain is trying to recover. What did the doctor say about overcoming this kind of amnesia?"

There was a knock at the door.

"Come in."

A dark-haired man stuck his head in the door. "Hi, Elbert."

Elbert smiled. "Ah, ask and ye shall receive." He stood up and shook the man's hand.

"Jenny, Bobby, this is Doctor Richard Maston. He's the head of surgery over at Wooster Community and he's also a clinical psychologist. I had him look in on Steven Lambright after the incident today. Rick, Jenny has a question about retrograde amnesia. You can speak to it better than I can."

The doctor shook hands with Jenny and Bobby and then pulled up another chair. "So how can I help you, Mrs...."

"Just Jenny, Doctor."

"Good. What was your question, Jenny?"

"Well, I just asked Elbert if the doctor said anything about overcoming this kind of amnesia? What did you call it? Oh, right, retrograde amnesia. You've examined Steven—what's your opinion?"

Doctor Maston pulled out a small notepad and scanned his notes. Then he looked up. "Well, Steven Lambright is a very unusual case. The actual surgery and not the injury causes most post trauma amnesia. Steven Lambright was struck a glancing blow by a fifty-caliber machine gun shell. To put it in layman's terms, it opened his skull and knocked him silly. Those battlefield hospitals didn't have the latest equipment, so during the surgical repair, there was some damage to the amygdala. This is the part of the brain that is involved in fear and fear memories. Its primary job is to regulate emotions such as fear and aggression. It plays a part in how memories are stored because stress hormones acting on the amygdala influence storage."

Jenny was also taking notes. "So, if someone suffered some traumatic experiences that involved great fear or aggression, that memory would be stored in the Amy... the Amy..."

Doctor Maston smiled. "The amygdala. Well, the amygdala plays a role in forming these memories. But the hippocampus then processes those memories and stores them in the prefrontal cortex. Let me give an example. One researcher experimented with rats and their fear. Using Pavlovian conditioning, he paired a neutral tone with a foot shock to the rats. This produced a fear memory in the rats. After this conditioning, each time they heard the tone, they would freeze, which is a defense response in rats, indicating a memory for the impending shock. Then the researchers induced cell death in neurons in the lateral amygdala, which is the specific area of the brain responsible for fear memories. They found the fear memory faded and eventually became extinct. It took a long time, though."

Bobby leaned forward. "So, what you are saying is that the injury to Steven Lambright's amygdala caused him to forget the fear memories that he had."

"Yes, that's exactly right."

"But why did he remember something that may have happened before he went to battle?"

"The amygdala forms those fear memories, but another part of the brain stores them. Steven's injury broke the connection to these memories, but they are still there inside his head somewhere. Many researchers believe strong emotions trigger strong memories. This is called arousal theory. The bigger the memory, the harder they are to forget."

Jenny looked down at her notes and then asked another question. "Because Steven Lambright had these strong fear emotions, first with the horrible death of his father, which he believed he caused, and then with whatever happened to him before he joined the army, and then the incredible shock and stress of seeing his friends killed and being shot in the head, could have caused powerful memories which might be buried somewhere in his brain?"

"And the damage to his amygdala has somehow blocked the transmittal of those memories to his conscious mind. Yes. At least that's how I see it. Most post-traumatic amnesia only lasts for a couple of days. It can last, in rare cases, for weeks or months. Steven Lambright has suffered from this amnesia since 1968. That's thirty-seven years."

Jenny furrowed her brow. "Why do you think it has lasted so long, Doctor?"

"Good question, Jenny. As a clinical psychologist, it is my belief that Steven Lambright has somehow blocked the ability of his memory to project information to his brain that gives his memories meaning and connects them with other related memories. The incredible fear and stress he experienced has short-circuited some of the normal healing processes in the brain."

"So, Steven's amnesia is due more to a blocking of information that interprets these memories and they are actually still there?"

"Exactly. Great stress triggers what we call flashbulb memories, an exceptionally clear recollection of an important event. The seizure that Steven Lambright suffered when you showed him the serial killer's signature triggered one of those flashbulb memories and it literally overwhelmed him with the re-experienced terror of some moment that occurred in his life that was incredibly stressful."

Elbert spoke up. "Why didn't he react to that signature in the courtroom?"

"You've spent time with Steven, Elbert. He is almost

completely disconnected from the world around him. I believe he just wasn't in the room mentally when the prosecutors presented that evidence. When they showed it to the jury, Lambright was in another world. At least, that's my opinion."

Jenny asked one more question. "Do you think something could restore those flashbulb memories?"

Doctor Maston sighed. "Another good question, Jenny. That could go one of two ways. If you pressed Steven too hard, he might just abandon the tenuous links that hold him to reality and go completely insane."

"And the other way?"

"Through some miracle, or possibly a real shock to his system—perhaps like he experienced today when he saw the 3 X 3 signature—he could regain normal function of his brain, remember and then process those memories, and from there, lead a completely normal life. But I believe it would have to be after some event eliminated the source of the terror and fear, so he felt safe in reprocessing the memories. My humble opinion."

Jenny looked at Bobby. "There is only one source for miracles that I know. And we definitely need one."

Bobby nodded and turned to Elbert. "So, what do you think about all this, Elbert?"

Elbert chuckled. "Jenny, you have the astounding ability to turn something that I hold to be simple as pie into something that will take some real cop work to straighten out." He grinned. "Do you do that on purpose?"

Jenny smiled. "Well, Elbert, when I met you, you were a detective upstairs sharing a space, and now you have a big office on the first floor."

Everyone chuckled. Elbert looked around and settled back in his chair. "True, Jenny. Very true."

Jenny and Bobby were back in Apple Creek after a long day. They were in the kitchen, where Jenny was making some poor man's steak and Bobby was enjoying some *Kaffee*. There was a knock at the front door, and then they heard it open.

"Mama? Mama, here we are!"

"Rachel!"

Jenny put down her spatula and headed for the door. "Don't let those burn, Bobby."

In a few minutes, Jenny led her daughter Rachel and Rachel's husband Daniel into the kitchen. Rachel's arms were full of packages and Daniel carried two suitcases.

Bobby started to get up, but Rachel put her packages on the table, sat down next to him, and gave him a kiss on the cheek. "Well, here we are. Daniel starts working with Christopher Mast soon, so we thought we would come and settle in. And I see that I'm just in time to help my culinary-challenged mother with dinner. Poor man's steak?"

Jenny nodded. "Yes, but it's almost ready, so *setzen sie sich*. I'm so glad you're here. Bobby's been tolerating my cooking, but I saw his face light up when he heard you come in the door and I know why."

Bobby looked sheepishly at Jenny. "Well, you don't do so badly, but we have been going to Der Dutchman restaurant a lot. Let's just say your talents lie in other areas. Yes, Rachel is indeed welcome. And Daniel, it's good to see you, my friend."

Daniel shook Bobby's hand. A look passed between them, the look men who have gone into battle or faced great danger together share.

"Yes, Uncle Bobby, glad to be here."

Jenny pointed to the hallway. "You know where your room is. Put your stuff in there and then come back for some *Kaffee.*"

In a few minutes, Daniel and Rachel were back. Jenny had already poured, and Daniel slid into the seat next to Bobby.

Bobby patted him on the shoulder. "You're starting to work with Chris Mast on your new Morgan horse farm?"

Daniel nodded. "Yes, and it's going to be a challenge. Chris and I have divergent ideas about breeding Morgan horses, and we will have to work together for a while to sort those out. But, fortunately, I really don't have to start for two weeks."

Jenny looked over from the stove. "Well then, you came down pretty early. Why the rush?"

Daniel grinned and looked at Rachel. "We heard you have another case going, and we thought maybe we could… you know… help."

Bobby nodded. "Timing is everything, my boy. We are just getting ready to search six hundred acres of wilderness out west of town. I'd love to have some company."

"You got it, Uncle Bobby."

Rachel put some cream in her *Kaffee.* "Tell us what's going on, Mama."

"Give me a minute," said Jenny, as she slid the baking dish with the evening's dinner into the oven. Once it was going, she came and sat down. "Well, Rachel, we have a serial killer in Wooster."

"In Wooster?" Rachel shook her head. "*Wozu kommt diese Welt?*"

"Indeed. What is it coming to? The killer murdered three women, randomly, it appeared. He left a signature at the scene of each crime, scratched into the skin of his victims with the tip of a very sharp knife. Everyone thought the killer was just a psychopath. Lieutenant Wainwright and his team followed some overly obvious clues and arrested a man named Steven Lambright. Steven is a Vietnam War veteran with retrograde amnesia—he remembers nothing before he was wounded in a terrible battle in Southeast Asia. All the evidence pointed straight to him."

Bobby unconsciously reached for a Camel, thought better of it, and then rubbed his chin in a thoughtful sort of way. "But your mother just couldn't get past the fact that Steven's mother swears he would kill no one—not again, not after what he did and saw in Vietnam."

Jenny took a sip. "And the interesting thing, Rachel, is that he grew up Amish. His father died in a farming accident and it profoundly affected his life. And then something happened to him when he was a teenager that terrified him. He ran away and joined the army. When he came home, he remembered nothing of his past life. So, I think he was the perfect candidate for a set up—somebody made it look like Steven did the killings. And one of the murdered women, Elizabeth Gingerich Ingersoll, also grew up in an Amish home, close to Steven. Their mothers said they both spent a lot of time in the woods between their houses. And the interesting thing is that something horrible happened to her, too, on the same day in 1967. I believe whatever this terrible event was, happened to both of them when they were together. I am going to find out what it was and uncover the connection between Steven Lambright and Liz Ingersoll."

Daniel had been silent. Finally, he spoke. "So, what you are looking for in the park is a place Steven and Elizabeth might have stayed when they were away from home?"

Bobby nodded. "Maybe in an outbuilding behind a farm or even something they built out in the woods."

"And if we could find somebody who knew about them being together or where they might have stayed, perhaps we could find out more about what happened."

Jenny nodded.

"Great!" said Daniel. "When do we start?"

# 16

# THE HIDING PLACE

*B*obby and Daniel were out checking houses on Ashland Road, across the highway from Wooster Park. Many of the farms along the route belonged to Amish people, so Daniel's presence opened some doors. They had been out for several hours, but after talking with four or five people, they became discouraged. No one had ever seen Elizabeth and Steven together, nor did they know of any hideouts in the woods. Most of the farmers were younger, and some had not even been born in 1966. The two men were thinking of driving over to Highway 250 on the other side of the park and checking there. Before they turned around, Daniel noticed a white mailbox at the head of a driveway partly concealed by thick forsythia bushes.

"Let's try down there, Bobby."

Bobby turned in and they followed the track for a long way off the road. Finally, it opened out into a circular driveway that went around a big house painted light blue. A wide porch ran all the way along the front of the two-story building and the entire house sat up on posts. Two bright red outbuildings surrounded by trees ablaze in fall colors completed the picture. A black Amish buggy sat in front of a large barn to the left and a smaller building that looked like a shop sat off to the right under some trees. Three chimneys poked out of the top of the house. As they pulled up, an older Amish man walked out of the house. Bobby stopped and turned off the motor, and he and Daniel climbed out.

The Amish man walked across the porch to the railing and leaned over. He saw Daniel was Amish and waved.

"*Wie geht es dir?*"

Daniel waved back. "*Sehr gut. Und wie geht es dir?*"

"*Gut, danke.*" The man motioned for them to come up. They walked up the steps. At the top, Daniel held out his hand, and the man shook it.

"Amos Starmer."

"Daniel King. And this is..."

Amos smiled. "*Ja, ja*, Sheriff Halverson. I know him. I voted for him five times. What brings you out here?"

Bobby shook Amos's hand and looked around. "Well, I'm kind of back in harness, Amos. I'm helping the Wooster police with a case."

"*Ja*, you and Jenny Hershberger. We all know about that. Jenny has helped the Amish people. I knew her papa."

"Reuben, you knew Reuben?"

Amos nodded. "A good man, such a tragedy when he died." Amos went to the front door and opened it. "*Kumme, kumme.* Mama has some *küchen* on the table, and hot *Kaffee.*"

They went inside. The house smelled of baked goods and roast beef. Amos led them to a bright functional kitchen. A small Amish woman was bustling about. She waved them to the table.

"*Setzen sie, setzen sie. Küchen? Kaffee?*"

Both men smiled and nodded. Amos pulled up a chair. "So, what are you doing out in our neck of the woods?"

Bobby waited while Mrs. Starmer poured the coffee. Then he spoke. "We are investigating the 3 X 3 murders."

Amos looked puzzled. "But I thought they arrested the man who did it."

Bobby shook his head. "The police thought so, but in the rush to judgment, we missed some information that has now surfaced and we felt we should look into it. So, we are going through this neighborhood asking some questions and looking for help."

"How can we help you?"

"Did you know that Steven Lambright grew up Amish?"

Amos nodded. "*Ja,* that's been going around the grapevine."

"What you probably didn't know was that one of the murdered women also grew up Amish. The woman known as Liz Ingersoll. Her maiden name was Elizabeth Gingerich, and she lived on Ashland Road."

Amos looked at his wife. "The Gingeriches? Just down the road?" Amos scowled. "*Ja, ja,* we knew them."

His wife stopped what she was doing and put her hands on her hip. "*Ja,* I knew Wanda... and Elizabeth—when she was a little girl. That husband of hers, Johan. He was a terrible man."

Bobby glanced at Daniel and then asked a question. "How do you mean, a terrible man?"

"He *vas* a *Sexualstraftäter...* one of those sex offenders. He molested Elizabeth. Wanda told me about it after he died. Of course, Elizabeth ran away forty years ago—because of what he was doing."

Daniel interjected. "The abuse was only part of it. What we found out from her mother was she ran away because of something terrible that happened right around the fourth of July in 1967. And here's the interesting part. Something happened to Steven Lambright on that same day that made him run away and join the army. And Jenny Hershberger, that's my wife's mother, thinks the same thing happened to both. She believes Steven and Elizabeth were involved in an event that terrified them so much they had to escape."

Amos pulled a pipe out of his pocket and tamped it, then lit it. He stared at his guests.

"Do you mind if I smoke, too?" asked Bobby.

Amos nodded. "So, you think Lambright and Elizabeth knew each other?"

Bobby pulled out a Camel, lit it, took a drag. "Yes. Steven Lambright lived on the other side of Wooster Park. When he was fourteen, his father was killed in a haying accident."

Amos's eyes opened wide. "Mervin Lambright. *Ja*. I remember that. *Schrecklich, schrecklich*."

"Steven's mother said Steven felt his father's death was his fault. She said he changed after that, became secretive, spent many hours, sometimes days, out in the park. And Elizabeth was also out there, avoiding her father's assaults. Jenny believes the two of them met and became friends. And they were together when something happened that changed their lives."

"That was a long time ago, Sheriff. What do you hope to find after all these years?"

Mrs. Starmer cut a piece of cake and looked at Daniel expectantly. He smiled and nodded yes as she slipped it onto his plate.

Daniel answered Amos. "Steven and Elizabeth were gone a lot out in the woods. Sometimes for days. We think they had a hiding place, somewhere Elizabeth's father could not find, and where Steven could deal with his ghosts. And we think it was either a little-used outbuilding behind a farm or something they may have built out in the woods."

Amos nodded. "*Ja, Ja*, there are many places out there that someone could hide. Lots of ravines, cliffs, caves... it could be anywhere. And there are many older farms along both sides of the park, farms that have buildings constructed even one hundred years ago. When the Spanglers turned the land over to the city in 1961, they gave almost five hundred acres, but there were many more acres next to the park that had gone back to the wild. The park has changed a lot, but forty years ago it was a wilderness."

"Gerhardt Müller."

Everyone turned to look at Mrs. Starmer.

"Gerhard Müller. He's lived by the park for at least thirty years. And he's been over every inch. If anybody knows anything, Gerhard would."

"And also, Granny Lengacher," said Amos. "She's lived on this road for eighty-five years. Born in her house just two miles from here. If anybody knows about the doings out in those woods, it would be Granny."

Bobby pulled out a notebook. "Got some addresses?"

***

GRANNY LENGACHER WAS OUT IN HER YARD, RAKING UP SOME early leaves, when Bobby and Daniel pulled in. Her house was tiny with a small covered front porch. Shingled sides painted light brown and a single narrow window in the house's front wall. The old woman looked up as Bobby and Daniel climbed out of the truck. She had snow white hair under her *kappe* and a warm coat covered her dress. She wielded her garden rake with authority.

Daniel doffed his hat. "*Guten Tag*, Mrs. Lengacher. I'm Daniel King and this is my friend, Sheriff Bobby Halverson."

"Retired sheriff," smiled Bobby.

"*Ja*, Sheriff Halverson. I remember. *Ich erinnere mich, dass Sie ein guter Freund der Amish waren.* You were well-liked by the plain people. How can I help you on this cold fall day?"

"We are helping the Wooster police with some recent crimes that involve Amish people that lived in this area, and our search has led us to you."

"Well, perhaps you should come in for some hot apple cider. I don't enjoy answering questions in the winter wind."

She led them inside. The old house reminded Bobby of a very upscale antique store. Everything was in perfect order. The table was handmade and polished to a high gleam. Knitted doilies covered the chair backs. There was a small wood-burning stove with a stack of wood neatly piled beside it.

Bobby looked around. "Your house is beautiful, Mrs. Lengacher. So well kept."

"Well, I'm not dead yet, so I just keep doing what has to be done. And call me Granny."

"Is there a Mister Lengacher?"

"He died a long time ago."

"Amos Starmer said you have lived in this house all your life."

She nodded. "*Ja.* I was born here on this land in 1917. This was the *dawdy haus*. The big house burned down after my husband died. Never got around to rebuilding it. What you see here is what I could salvage after the fire. Now you said your investigation has led you to me. In what way?"

She motioned for them to sit at the small kitchen table and then went to the stove. The smell of hot apple cider permeated the kitchen. She got two more cups from the cupboard and ladled some cider into them. "The old saying is, 'an apple a day keeps the doctor away,' and so I drink mine. Seems to work."

"What we need to find out is if you know two people that lived in this area about forty years ago and, if so, what you know about them."

"Which people?"

"Kids actually. They would have been in their teens when they were here. They spent a lot of time out in the woods, in the park. We think they spent it together."

"Names?"

"Steven Lambright and Elizabeth Gingerich."

Granny nodded. "*Ja*, Steven and Lizzie. I knew them."

Bobby looked over at Daniel.

*Pay dirt!*

"Have you heard about the murders in Wooster?"

"A little. Not much, though. I don't go out at all and I don't take the papers."

"Three women were murdered in Wooster. Elizabeth Gingerich was one of them and the police have arrested Steven Lambright."

"What? Steven?"

"Yes. But we, that is Lieutenant Wainwright and I and Jenny Hershberger, don't think Steven did it."

Granny scowled. "He couldn't have done it. Not Steven. He loved Elizabeth. Not romantically, but like a sister, you know. They used to come here when they were hungry. I caught them stealing eggs from my chicken house one day. I was going out to fetch some eggs and there they were. I could see they were hungry, so I let them go."

"Do you know where they went?"

"No, I never figured it out. They were like little deer. They would go into the woods and disappear."

"After that first day, did they come back?"

"Yes, about a week later they were back and this time they brought some money to pay for the eggs. I told them to keep their money and took them inside for breakfast. After that, I saw them every few days. I think they felt safe here."

Bobby pressed in. "What can you tell us about them?"

"Well, Steven was a gentle boy, but he carried such a weight. When his father died, it nearly broke him. Steven was helping in the harvest, and he wasn't paying attention to what he was doing. He almost walked into a thresher, but his father jumped in and pushed him out of the way. The thresher caught his father's coat and pulled him in. A terrible way to die and Steven saw it."

"And what about Elizabeth?"

Granny looked out the window for a moment and sighed. "Ah, poor Lizzie. Her father... well, he was a bad'un. He abused her. That's why she spent so much time away from her home. She was terrified of him."

Daniel nodded. "And how old were they when you met them?"

"I'd say Steven was sixteen or seventeen, Lizzie the same. I saw a lot of them for several months but then they started going in to town. They were older, and it was their rumspringa and they wanted to see what life in the *Englischer* world was like."

"So, the two of them were very close?"

"Two? Did I say two? No, no, there were three of them. Steven, Lizzie and Aldon. They were always together."

Bobby leaned forward. "Three of them? Steven and Lizzie and Aldon? Who is Aldon?"

"Aldon Lehman. He was an Amish boy whose family had a big farm along the highway over on the other side of the park. They met each other out there, and after that, they were inseparable. They built a little place out in the woods. It was their secret hideout."

"Three of them. Do you know where this place was?"

"No, they never told me. They told no one."

"Where is this Aldon now?"

"Oh, he died about thirty years ago. Killed in a car wreck. Got burned up."

Bobby looked at Daniel. "This is very interesting. Three of them. Anything else you can tell us, Granny?"

The old woman puzzled for a moment. Then her face brightened. "Yes, I told you they had a secret hideout in the woods. They had sort of a club out there, a secret society they called it, very hush-hush. They swore themselves to always be together, like a blood oath. Let's see, it had a strange symbol. Oh, I remember..."

She got a pencil and a piece of paper. "Lizzie showed it to me, but she made me swear I wouldn't tell the boys." She drew something on the paper and then lifted it.

"This is it."

Daniel and Bobby stared down at the paper.

3 X 3.

## SECRETS

*J*enny looked up from the drawing Bobby and Daniel brought from Granny Lengacher's house. "I think we may be getting to the bottom of all this."

Rachel was sitting next to her mother. "So, there were three kids out in the woods, not two. And they called themselves 3 X 3. Did Granny Lengacher say anything about this Aldon..."

"Lehman," Bobby said. "Yes. She told us that Aldon Lehman's family was one of the wealthiest in Wayne County. They had a large farm out past her house."

"Was there something that happened to Aldon, like with Steven and Elizabeth?"

Bobby shook his head. "As far as Granny knew, the Lehmans were a normal Amish family. But both of Aldon's parents died when Aldon was just barely twenty and he inherited the farm. Granny said after his parents died mysteriously, Aldon took to drinking. But less than a year later, he left the Amish faith and sold the farm to an *Englischer,*

Gerhardt Müller. Then, shortly after, he died in a car wreck. He ran off the road and the car burst into flame. Not much left of him."

Jenny looked down at the drawing again. "But somehow, before what happened in 1967, he became very close with Lizzie and Steven."

Daniel nodded. "Yes. Granny said that she never saw them apart until Steven and Lizzie started *Rumspringa.* Then she would see just the two of them. She thought maybe Aldon's parents were cracking down and he couldn't get away so much."

"Then what happened?" Jenny asked.

"Granny said one day she saw Lizzie and Steven without Aldon. They were going into Wooster to attend some kind of festival. That was in May. She saw them a few times after that and then, around the fourth of July, they both just vanished. Aldon never came back to her house, either. Much later, she heard that Lizzie had run away and Steven had joined the army. And not long after that, Aldon died. She thought that Lizzie finally had enough of her father and left, and Steven, lost without his best friend, just took off. But that was mostly conjecture on her part."

"And you said the Starmers suggested we look up Gerhard Müller."

Daniel looked over. "Yes. They said he knew the woods better than anyone, and could probably find the hideout for us. He also owns the Lehman farm, so there may be some clues out there. Oh, and one last thing. Granny said the word was Aldon sold the farm long distance. Gerhard Müller lived in New York, and he didn't actually move out to the farm until after Aldon died."

Jenny looked up with a puzzled look on her face. "No one

met Müller until he moved to the farm after Aldon Lehman's death?"

Bobby nodded. "Granny didn't, that's for sure. In fact, she told us she has never met Müller. He's a real loner. He only hires *Englischers* who live in town and even they don't see him much. He leaves their pay in his barn. We could check with the Starmers and see if they know him. He seems like a pretty reclusive character."

"Whew! This story is getting more convoluted every minute."

"What are you going to do, Mama?" Rachel asked.

"Talk to Elbert. I think we need to go visit Gerhard Müller and see if he can help us find the hideout."

———

GERHARD MÜLLER WAS NOT AT HOME WHEN JENNY, BOBBY, and Daniel came to visit. They looked around in admiration when they drove down the long driveway and climbed out of the truck. The old Lehman place was a stunner. The paint on the barn was fresh and the gingerbread trim above the large house-wrapping veranda was immaculately detailed. The property records they looked up before they came told the story. The property enclosed three hundred acres bordering on Wooster Park. Müller grew feed corn and hay there. An extensive field of dry brown corn, ready to be cut, rustled in the fall wind and covered the rolling hills all around the property. A large fenced-in garden occupied the space between the house and the out-buildings. As they climbed out of the truck, they heard horses whinnying in the barn. A man in overalls was using a rototiller in the garden, obviously getting ready for spring planting, but when they walked up and asked if he was Gerhard Müller, he shook his head.

"Nope. Wish I was, but I ain't. Gerhard is out in the woods. I'm the hired man. I come in once or twice a month to do the heavy lifting."

Jenny smiled. "Do you know when he will be back?"

The man shook his head. "Nope. He's a wanderer. Somethin' about those woods that draws him. He probably knows more about Wooster Park than any living Ohio native, that's for sure. I just show up and look at the list he leaves for me in the barn. I don't see him much."

"What about harvest? Who does the work then?"

"Oh, I help and he hires crews to do the work. He gets them to do most of the work by hand—doesn't use a lot of machinery."

Jenny looked around. "That's interesting. Is he Amish?"

"Nah. He's one of those greenies, you know, an environmentalist. Plus, he's got more money than you can shake a stick at, so he can afford to pay them to work longer. He wants to be more in tune with nature, he says, so he tries to use these green methods around the place."

Daniel took in the place with a glance. "Seems to work."

"Well, would you mind telling Mr. Müller we were here?" Bobby asked.

The man nodded. "Shore. I'll leave a note... say, won't have to. You can tell him yourself." The hand pointed toward the woods. A tall man with a neatly trimmed beard was coming out of the woods. He wore camo clothing, a baseball cap, and carried a walking stick. The three of them waited while he walked up. He looked around as though he were checking for something, then focused on his visitors.

"Can I help you?" He said, curtly. His eyes moved from Jenny to Bobby to Daniel and back to Jenny.

Jenny stepped forward. "Mr. Müller?"

"Yes. What's this about?"

"I'm Jenny Hershberger. This is Sheriff Bobby Halverson and my son-in-law, Daniel King. We are working with Lieutenant Wainwright of the Wooster Police Department on a case of local concern."

"Oh, the murders?"

Jenny watched a strange expression cross the man's face. "Yes, how did you know?"

"Oh, everybody knows about you, Mrs. Hershberger. You're quite the local celebrity. Solving that case—the girl in the box, and then the Wittmer boy. I understand you're a real historian. So naturally, I assumed you are working on the Lambright case."

Jenny nodded. "Yes."

"Why? The man is guilty as sin. The evidence all points to him. And that's what the jury will find, I'm sure."

"Well, we aren't so sure of that as you seem to be, Mr. Müller. In fact, we are here because some very interesting information has surfaced that may put the kibosh on the whole trial. And we only have a few days to see if we are right. That's why we need your help."

"My help? What can I do?"

"One of the murdered women actually grew up in an Amish family right down the road from here. Elizabeth Gingerich, known to most people as Liz Ingersoll. And it has also surfaced that she and Steven Lambright, and the man who sold you this farm, Aldon Lehman, were very close as teenagers."

"Who told you that?"

"Granny Lengacher."

Müller laughed. "That old looney? Boy, if you believe her, I have a bridge to sell you."

"What makes you say that?"

"I've lived around here for thirty years and Granny Lengacher is well known in these parts. Never leaves that place, runs people off who come on her land…"

"Do you know her personally?"

"Well… not really. I've never met her, but I know what the talk around here is."

"Granny told us that Steven and Lizzie and Aldon were very close and that Steven would never hurt Lizzie."

"I wouldn't know about all that. You see, I never even met Aldon Lehman before I bought this place. I saw it in a real estate magazine in New York and had my agents do the whole deal. By the time I moved here, Lehman was dead. And I never heard of those other people. Now, I'm a busy man. You said I could help you. In what way?"

"Well, Mr. Müller, you have your own reputation around these parts. Mrs. Starmer told us you know Wooster Park and the woods around it like the back of your hand. And that's how you can help us. You see, the three of them, Lizzie, Steven, and Aldon, had a hiding place, kind of a clubhouse, somewhere in the woods. A place where they went to, a secret place."

"Out in the park?"

"Yes, Mr. Müller, out there somewhere."

Müller shook his head. "Well, Mrs. Starmer is right. I know these woods well. But I have never found any place like that." He paused. "Not to say it couldn't be there. I haven't covered every inch of ground in those woods. A great deal of what we see depends on what we are looking for."

Jenny glanced over at Müller. "Are you from an Amish background, Mr. Müller?"

"No, why do you ask?"

"Well, you have a name that comes from German or Swiss roots. It just struck me."

Müller laughed. "No, I never even knew any Amish back in New York. I find them a rather odd group of people…" He smiled at Jenny, but it was a wintry smile. "No offense meant, Mrs. Hershberger."

"None taken, Mr. Müller."

"I do little socializing here in Ohio. I like my privacy, Mrs. Hershberger. My parents were wealthy from a very old New England family. I led a very sheltered life."

"I understand, Mr. Müller, and I don't want to put pressure on you, but a man's life is at stake. Would there be a possibility that you could show us some of the woods, maybe take us to places you haven't been and help us answer our questions? If what Granny says is true, then it could change the whole direction of this case. And if not, then we could lay our concerns to rest."

Müller looked at his three visitors. "Well, I'm a very busy man. I have my own life to live."

"If you could just give us a day, we would be very grateful. The trial is going to wind up soon, and if the jury finds Steven Lambright guilty or even insane, he will face sentencing shortly after that. We have little time."

Müller was silent for a moment. Then he sighed. "All right. We'll give it one day. Meet me here tomorrow at 7:00 a.m. sharp." He looked at Jenny. "And I would recommend wearing something besides that dress. Some places in the woods are pretty rough."

Jenny smiled sweetly. "Believe me, Mr. Müller, I've been out in the woods in this dress many times. I might surprise you."

"As you will, Mrs. Hershberger."

"Jenny. Please call me Jenny."

Eldon and Gary sat in the courtroom. The jury had been out for three hours. The defense attorney had made a last-minute desperate plea to back up her insanity defense, and Elbert saw it swayed some of the jury members.

"So, what if they buy the insanity defense?" asked Gary.

"Then the Judge will have to commit Lambright to a mental institution. After the jury finds someone not guilty by reason of insanity, they are sent to a state-run psychiatry facility for a short period to be evaluated. The doctors decide if they need long-term treatment. Most times, the answer to this question is 'yes'. However, it's conceivable that someone could have had a temporary condition, and the doctors may rule that they are no longer insane."

"Oh, like back in the seventies in San Francisco when Dan White killed Mayor Moscone and Harvey Milk? Didn't the jury let him off because he said he ate too many Twinkies and it made him temporarily crazy? The Twinkie defense?"

Elbert chuckled. "Yeah, something like that. But in this case, Lambright is a wounded Vietnam Vet who obviously was mentally and physically damaged in combat. His attorney did an excellent job of bringing that out. So, I'd say he's got a good chance of getting off on insanity."

"Then what?"

"Well, because he is so damaged, I would think that he would be in an institution for the rest of his life."

Just then, there was a stir in the court.

The bailiff stood and spoke as the judge entered. "All rise."

Everyone stood. The judge sat down and then so did they. The judge looked over at the bailiff. "Bailiff, please bring in the prisoner and recall the jury. I believe they've reached a verdict."

There was a stir among the people in the room.

The bailiff nodded to the guards, who left the room. In a moment, they brought a very confused-looking Steven Lambright back into the courtroom. He wore an orange jail jumpsuit and there were shackles on his wrists. He sat down where the guards told him. In another moment, the jury room door opened, and the jury filed in. As soon as they found their seats, the judge spoke to the foreman, who stood facing him.

"Has the jury reached a verdict?"

"We have, Your Honor."

The judged turned to Steven Lambright. "Will the defendant please rise,"

Steven looked around. The guard behind him nudged him to his feet.

"Mr. Foreman, what is your verdict?"

"We find the defendant, Steven Lambright, not guilty by reason of insanity."

There was a cry in the courtroom and a rumble of conversation. The judge pounded his gavel, and the room quieted.

"So say you all?"

"Yes, Your Honor. So say we all."

The judge looked down at Steven. "Steven Lambright, because you have been found criminally insane, I must remand you to a facility for evaluation, prior to your sentencing. Therefore, I remand you to the Central Ohio Behavioral Healthcare Center for observation and to confirm the depth of your treatment and incarceration, if needed. This court is adjourned."

Elbert and Gary stood while the judge left, and the room

cleared. The bailiff and the two guards led Steven Lambright away. On a back bench, surrounded by several Amish people, Mrs. Lambright wept.

"Well, it's good for her," said Elbert. "I like her and this is a good thing, probably the best for Steven. At least it keeps him from being executed."

Gary nodded. "And it gives Jenny more time to see if she can dig something up."

Elbert smiled. "So now you're a believer?"

"Well, the more you know, the more you know you don't know."

"That's an Amish saying."

Gary blushed. "Yeah. I learned it from Jenny."

## 18

# IN THE WOODS

*J*enny, Bobby, and Daniel showed up at the Müller place at 7:00 a.m. Gerhard Müller was waiting for them. He glanced at his wristwatch and nodded.

"Right on time. Thank you. Follow me."

He turned and walked toward the woods. Bobby and Jenny were right behind him, and Daniel stayed back a little.

Müller led them into an open meadow surrounded by woods. He led the way along the upper edge of the field until they came to a well-marked trail. He swept his arm, taking in the open space.

"This area is called The Field. This is the Old Field Trail. I think the Spanglers had some crops in here before they turned it over to the city. This trail is medium difficulty."

They crossed the field on the trail and then came to a junction.

Müller stopped and waited for them to catch up. "This is the Education Trail. A lot of the schools in the area bring their kids here for field trips. If you turn left, the trail runs along the edge of the woods. It's very open, not really any places that could be hidden there, so we'll go right."

They followed the trail into the woods. It wound around through the trees. Ahead, they heard the rushing of a creek. They came down to a small stream. Trees clothed in fall colors closed in above them. Müller halted.

"Most of the creeks out here are part of the Apple Creek watershed. This one runs out of the park and down through Grosjean Park on the other side of Wooster. From there it flows into Killbuck Creek, down to the Wahonding River, and from there into the Ohio." He turned and went ahead. Jenny called to him.

"Mr. Müller?"

He stopped and turned back. "Yes?"

"These trails, Mr. Müller, they seem to be very easy and quite out in the open. Perhaps we should look deeper in the park, along some more difficult trails."

Müller got a look of exasperation on his face. "Very well, Mrs... Jenny. I was just trying to make things a little easier for you."

"I'm just fine, Mr. Müller. Lead on."

They started off again. Jenny turned to Bobby and whispered. "How are you doing?"

Bobby grinned. "No worse than the jungles of Guadalcanal."

"You were a little younger then, Bobby."

"I'm good, Jenny. If I collapse, Daniel can just drag me back to that field and bury me there."

They both chuckled. "No, really Jenny. I am good."

Daniel came up. "I'm watching out for him, Mama."

"Coming?" Müller was waiting. "We'll go back and hit the Spangler Trail. That leads to the Outer Trail. That's where the wildest part of the park is. Hope you can keep up."

"Actually. Mr. Müller, we are fine."

Müller turned and strode off.

---

IN ABOUT HALF AN HOUR, THEY CAME TO THE JUNCTION OF TWO trails. Beyond them was a small pond. Müller pointed to the left. "This is the Outer Trail. It runs along the northern boundary of the park. We'll go north for a bit and then turn east. From there, we will go through the densest part of the park. I have done much walking here, but I still don't know every bit back here."

Jenny nodded. "May I ask something of you, Mr. Müller?"

"What is that, Jenny?"

"On this part of the trail, we will look for places that could conceal the hiding place we are hoping to find. So instead of just strolling through here, perhaps we can slow the pace and be a little more observant of our surroundings?"

It was clear from the look on his face that Müller did not like to take directions. Jenny spoke up. "I know this is a bother for you, Mr. Müller, and I promise, if you can just bear with us for a few more hours, we will be out of your hair and we will go on our way. Does that work for you?"

Müller sighed. "That's fine, Jenny. I won't borrow trouble from tomorrow."

Jenny watched Müller as he turned and led them up the path. She had a quizzical look on her face.

Soon they were in the deep woods. The trees closed in all around them and the brush crowded the trail. They came into a more open area with tall pines all along the trail, and then they crossed another creek. At one point, they had to force their way through some brush that crowded right up to the trail. Bobby, walking just behind Jenny, glanced down. A very faint trail split off under some brush and trailed away. Bobby called to Jenny. "Look at this."

Müller stopped, turned, and walked back. "What did you find?"

Bobby pointed. "An old trail leading off into the woods. Hasn't been used much."

"How did you see that, Sheriff?"

"Well, Mr. Müller, I was a member of a sniper patrol in the heart of the Guadalcanal jungle back in World War Two. They trained us to find Japanese hideouts. The Japanese were very good at sneaking through the woods on that island. There were bogs and swamps, trackless wastes, and rugged mountains. And that's where they hid. Compared to them, this one stood out like it had a road sign on it."

Müller looked closer. "It looks like it's been used before, but not for a while."

"Since 1967, perhaps?" asked Jenny.

"Perhaps."

"Do you know what's up there, Mr. Müller?"

"Not much, I'm afraid. The boundary of the park is just ahead and there are just a lot of steep banks leading up to higher ground and then private property."

"Just what we are looking for. Lead on, Mr. Müller."

They bent down under the brush and pushed through, following the trail. It wound faintly through the trees for a short way, then meandered through a maze of rocks and came to an area where it went left and right along the face of a very steep bank. The left-hand split went forward about ten feet and then came to a very brushy area at the base of a cliff and stopped. The group looked around and then turned to the right. The trail went over very rough ground and then through some more pines, across a creek and out into the open, where it joined back in with a very defined trail.

"This is the Outer Trail again," said Müller. "I've never been that way before. What say we walk on ahead. We will cross Rathburn Run, connect to the Trillum Trail and head back to my place from there. Does that sound good?"

Jenny nodded. "Well, I think so, Mr. Müller. It looks like there are not that many places to build a hiding place like we are looking for." They headed down the trail.

LATER, BACK AT THE APPLE CREEK HOUSE, JENNY, BOBBY, Daniel, and Rachel sat around the table in the kitchen drinking *Kaffee.*

Bobby was rubbing his knee. "A little creaky after that walk. Oh, to be young again..."

Jenny looked over at Bobby. "There is something not copacetic about Mr. Müller."

"What makes you say that?" asked Bobby.

"Just a few things I noticed. I will tell you if, and when, I figure all this out."

Bobby nodded. "Well, he certainly was not helpful. It was almost as if he were keeping us away from certain areas. When I found that faint trail back to the cliffs, he did not look happy at all."

"Yes," said Daniel. "And he got us out of that area as fast as he could. Besides that, he was rude to Jenny. I wanted to punch his face."

Rachel looked at her husband in shock. "Daniel!"

"I didn't do it, but it's not a sin to think it."

Just then, Bobby's phone chirped. Bobby answered. "Halverson." There was a pause. "What? When?"

There was more conversation from the other end. Then Bobby answered. "Wow. Yes, we will come right over." He clicked the phone off and looked at the faces around the table.

"What, Bobby?"

"Granny Lengacher is dead. They found her in her well. Elbert wants us to come over."

BOBBY AND JENNY LISTENED AS ELBERT TALKED TO A YOUNG man in a postal uniform.

"So, tell me again what happened."

The young man swallowed hard, obviously upset. "I came this morning to drop of the mail. Granny doesn't get much, but sometimes there are some ads, or junk mail, and I use that as an excuse."

"Excuse?"

"Yeah. Granny always has some cake and hot cider for me when I come. But today was different. When I drove up, the place was quiet. It's fall, and getting colder. Granny always has a fire going in her kitchen stove this time of year. But there was no smoke from the chimney. I pulled up and went to the front door. When I knocked, there was no answer. That's when I knew something was wrong."

"How's that?" asked Elbert.

"Granny never ever leaves this place, except on very special occasions and on Sunday, when her neighbors come and take her to church. She's so independent, but everybody loved her. And so predictable. The man from the grocery store always comes out to deliver on the same day of the week because she always needs the same things. So, no fire and no answer."

"What happened then?"

"I thought I better look around. She's getting old and something might have happened. I looked all around the place. Nothing."

"Then what?"

"I was walking past the well and I saw that a couple of bricks were missing from the edging. Granny keeps... Granny keeps this place up all the time. She can do mortar work and brick-laying. She never would have left the bricks missing from that edge. So, I looked over the edge and I saw something down in the well. It was dark, so I went to my truck and got a flashlight. I went back to the well and looked in." the young man paused, and wiped his eyes.

"There she was, her legs sticking up out of the water at the bottom. It was terrible. Poor old thing." The young man began to cry.

Jenny put her arm around him. "There, there. It's all right."

Elbert motioned for a uniformed officer. When his officer came up, he pointed to the mailman. "Take Jerry and get a full statement." The officer nodded and took Jerry off.

A man approached. Elbert introduced him. "This is Doctor Sherry. He's my medical guy. What's the word, John?"

The doctor shook his head. "Granny did not fall down the well and drown. There was no water in her lungs. She was dead before she hit the water."

"Did she hit her head on the way down?"

"A few slight bumps, Lieutenant, but not enough to kill her. No, she was strangled first and then pushed down the well. Granny Lengacher was murdered." The doctor held something up. "This was clutched in her hand."

It was a piece of cloth, torn off the sleeve of a coat.

"Granny fought her attacker." Jenny looked at Elbert. "And I've seen a coat like this before."

19

## THE PAST SPEAKS

Jenny Hershberger tossed and turned in her bed. Dark memories crowded into her dreams...

*She hobbled down the path, leaning on the heavy stick. The nylon line she wrapped around her leg and the branch to splint it was strong, and it supported the broken pine branch against her still throbbing ankle.*

*Suddenly, she stepped on a hidden rock, rolled her bad ankle, and pitched forward into the snow. The pain was agonizing. She tried to get up and realized she was going to have a hard time going any farther. She looked around for a place to hide. The light from the sun was slowly illuminating the sky. Ahead of her was a clump of bushes, and it was darker behind them. She poked the pine stick into the bushes, and instead of the wall of the ravine, her stick encountered... nothing!*

*A cave!*

*Jenny knew she had to hide somewhere, but her tracks would give her away. Then she remembered something Uncle Bobby had told her about hiding from the Japanese when he was a scout in the Marines.*

*"We would walk out to a place where the ground was hard and made our tracks hard to see and then walk backward in our tracks until we came to where we wanted to hide," he had told her. "Then we would jump off the trail and walk backward using a branch to sweep our tracks away. The enemy often walked right by where we were hiding and lost us. Some of the Indian guys from Arizona taught us that in sniper training."*

*Up ahead, the ravine narrowed, and the snow had not covered the trail because of the brush overhanging it. Jenny broke a branch off a Scotch broom and walked up the trail until there was no more snow. She stepped out onto the hard trail and took a few steps. Then she stepped backward as carefully as she could in her tracks until she came to the bush that hid the mouth of the cave. She gathered her strength and jumped off the trail.*

*Again, an agonizing pain shot up her leg. She gritted her teeth and inched backward into the bush, sweeping her tracks as she went. She pushed through and found the cave. It had a narrow, low entrance, but it looked big enough for her to wriggle through. She knelt down and crawled in...*

JENNY WOKE UP. THE CAVE WHERE SHE HID WHEN SHE RAN away with Jonathan, such a vivid dream. Why had she dreamed about the cave? And then her father's note came back to her, and the quiet voice in her heart... *Yes, Jenny, the past can tell us a lot.*

She sat up in bed. Everything fell into place in her head —all her questions, all the little clues, the anomalies. It all made perfect sense. And she knew who the killer was. She got up, lit a lamp, and found a pencil and a notepad. She sat on her bed and made a list. She checked it over. Satisfied that she had everything she needed to do in the morning, she went to her bed and crept in. She turned her lamp down. Before she closed her eyes, she whispered into the dark...

"Thank you, Papa."

---

Lieutenant Elbert Wainwright looked up at the little Amish woman and then down at the list of requests in his hand.

"Wow, Jenny, where did this all come from?"

"It's a long story, Elbert, and it started when I found a letter my papa hid in my writing desk years ago. When I read it, I realized the past can tell us a lot. And it reminded me of Jasper Jamison."

"Jasper Jamison?"

"Yes, he's a plumber in the village of Apple Creek. He was always poor and then one day he got a letter telling him he had inherited a great deal of money from a very distant relative, except they needed proof that he was indeed the Jasper Jamison mentioned in the will. Well, he did not know how to prove it, since he did not even know who this relative was, until, really for no reason, he remembered a chest his grandmother put away in the attic of his house before she died. He dug through a lot of stuff in the attic until he found the chest. And do you know what he found in the chest?"

Elbert shook his head. "I don't have the faintest idea."

"He found a family genealogy printed by hand on a roll of shelf paper. It went all the way back to his great-great-great-grandfather and showed all his relatives on both sides of the family, among whom was the very distant cousin who had left him the money. He was able to use it to prove he was the heir. And so Jasper found out that the past can tell us a lot."

"And that relates to this case in what way?"

"Did you see request number three?"

"Yes, and I can't do a disinterment unless there is an excellent reason to do so."

"Well, I am about to go about finding one."

---

JENNY AND BOBBY STOOD ON THE PORCH OF A NICE, comfortable looking bungalow on the outskirts of Dalton. Nicely kept roses were putting out their very last blooms of the season along the front of the house. A big buckeye tree graced the yard and the cape cod style of the building fit in nicely in the surrounding neighborhood. Jenny rang the bell again. The door opened and a white-haired man looked out.

"Yes?"

"Dr. Mansfield?"

"Yes."

"I'm Jenny Hershberger. I called earlier."

"Yes, yes, come in, Mrs. Hershberger."

"Jenny is fine, Doctor."

"And this is?"

"This is retired Sheriff Bobby Halverson."

The doctor's eyes lit up. "Of course. Bobby Halverson. A great sheriff. Those were good days in Wayne County."

Jenny thought she saw Bobby blush, and she grinned. The doctor showed them in to a very comfortable living room. "Can I get you anything, Jenny, Bobby?"

Jenny looked at Bobby, who held his stomach and shook his head. "No, thank you, Doctor. We just came from lunch at Der Dutchman. I don't think we'll be eating for a couple of days."

"Great place. Go there often myself. Now, what can I help you with?"

"The couple I asked you about?"

"Yes. Gerald and Eliza. They were good friends. Still a mystery to me why they died."

"What exactly were the circumstances, Doctor?" Bobby asked.

"Well, it was the winter of 1967. There was a terrible epidemic of the flu that year, all across Ohio. Gerald and Eliza came down with it and I treated them. They were sick, but they got through the rough part and were well on their way to recovery. And then I got a call from their son that they had both died. I couldn't understand it."

Jenny leaned forward. "Did you suspect anything, even foul play perhaps?"

The doctor got a strange look on his face. "Strange that you should ask that. I had a bad feeling about the whole thing. I didn't like their son. He seemed strange to me— pushy, demanding, spoiled, always very rude."

"Did you request an autopsy?"

"They were Amish. You know how the Amish are about autopsies. They don't allow them and it takes a lot of push to get them to go along. The son prepped their bodies, they lay in state in their home for three days and then they were in the ground and there was nothing I could do."

Jenny nodded. "Yes, it's hard to get the Amish to agree to an autopsy. Now I have a question. Do you still feel something strange happened with their deaths, strange enough to sign a request for disinterment?"

Dr. Mansfield looked at Jenny. "Absolutely."

JILL ABRAMS, THE HEAD OF THE JOHNSON TITLE COMPANY, looked at the paperwork for the property in question. She glanced over the front page and then folded over and read each of the following pages. Finally, she looked up. "This is an unusual sale. The property was purchased by a trust set up by a Müller family in New York State. The trustees are listed as Jonathan Müller, Rita Müller, and Gerhard Müller. The property was under-valued when Aldon Lehman sold it to the trust. Mr. Lehman did not use an agent but instead had an out-of-state law firm facilitate the sale, which is unusual for a local property. The title was transferred to Aldon Lehman upon the death of his parents, so he was the rightful owner. The payment was in cash and the fees were paid at the time of sale, and the deed transferred. This company did the title search and everything was clear, no encumbrances. I was not an officer of the company, but my father was. In fact, he was the one who did the chain of title search and the property survey. He provided the title insurance, established that Aldon Lehman held a clear title, managed the closing, and organized the cash transfer. It was only two months after the sale that Mr. Lehman died in a horrible car wreck. His car ran off a narrow road, crashed down a cliff, and exploded."

"Were you working here, then?"

Jill smiled. "Yes. I was going to Wooster College working on an accounting degree. I worked here as a summer intern learning the ropes, so I remember when all that happened."

"Did you ever meet Aldon Lehman?"

"No, and that's the odd part. No one here ever met Aldon Lehman, or any member of the Müller family during the sale. Attorneys facilitated the whole transaction.

And it was over five months after Aldon's death that Gerhard Müller came to Wooster and took possession. His attorney came into the office and picked up the paperwork. Müller had his signatures notarized, and we gave him his title."

"Can we ask you one more thing, Jill?"

"Certainly."

Jenny slid a piece of paper over. "Can you run a check on this entity? I need to know who really set it up and if it still exists. If it is legitimate and still exists, I would like the names of the trustees."

Jill looked down at the paper. "That will take a bit of work. This whole transaction goes back quite a way." She looked up. "But it piques my interest, so I am glad to do it for you."

Jenny stood up. "Thank you, Jill. You have been very helpful."

* * *

THREE DAYS LATER, JENNY, ELBERT, AND DANIEL WALKED UP the outer trail toward the spot where Bobby had found the faint trail leading toward the cliffs. After a twenty-minute walk, Daniel, who was in the lead, held up his hand.

"I think it was just ahead, Jenny, in that thick brush."

They went forward into the brush, looking for the faint trail.

"Here it is," said Daniel, pointing down.

The trail led away to the left under the brush. They pushed through to the other side. Here, the trail was more distinct. They followed it through the pines until they came to the stand of boulders. They made their way through them until they reached the cliff. Jenny pointed with the walking stick she was carrying. "Let's look along the face of the cliff to the left, behind the brush."

Elbert scratched his head. "What inspired you to come back to look here?"

Jenny smiled. "When I met my husband, Jonathan, we fell madly in love. My papa would not hear of me marrying outside the faith. So, we ran away together. What I didn't know was that Jonathan had been involved in a drug deal gone wrong back in San Francisco and he had ended up with a lot of money that belonged to a very bad bunch of crooks. He escaped from the situation and came east, hoping to get back to long Island to hide with his family. He ended up in Wooster, Ohio, and almost ran me over when I walked in front of his van. When we ran away, we got to Pennsylvania and then the crooks caught us."

Elbert shook his head. "And to think the first time I met you I thought you were a little old Amish grandmother who had no idea what the real world was like."

Jenny laughed. "I escaped from the crooks and I was running through the woods. I desperately needed a place to hide. I was thinking I would hide behind some brush along a creek bed. When I poked my stick in to find a place, it went all the way in and I found a cave behind some brush. I dreamed about that cave the other night and remembered the past can tell us a lot."

"And when Müller led us in a different direction, it raised my suspicions, too," said Daniel.

Jenny walked along the cliff, poking with her stick. "So, I believe we will find Steven and Lizzie's hideout somewhere... along... here."

The stick thrust through the brush and Jenny's arm followed almost to her wrist. "There's an opening through here!" said Jenny.

Elbert raised his hand. "Okay, let's do this carefully. I believe that someone who is deeply involved in this case knows about this place, so we must make sure we don't let them know we have been here. Be careful where you step." He pointed down. There was a faint boot track in the gravel. "We don't want to leave one of those."

Very gently, they pushed through the brush, stepping on the hard-packed dirt and gravel. In front of them was a narrow crack where a small ravine went back into the face of the cliff. The crack ended in a flat wall a step ahead of them. Set into the wall was a small wooden door. It was framed into the face of the cliff and stoutly made. Carved into the door was a symbol.

3 X 3.

# THE TRUTH WILL SET YOU FREE

*E*lbert stared at the door in amazement. It had an old-fashioned door knob with a keyhole under it. Elbert carefully tried the knob. Locked! He motioned for Jenny and Daniel to follow him. They stepped away from the cliff, pushed through the brush, and walked down the trail. Several yards away, Elbert halted them. He looked back toward the now hidden door.

"So, that is the hideout that Granny told us about and that is what got her killed. It looks like they spent a lot of time fixing the place up. And judging from that boot print, someone has been here lately. It rained three nights ago and that track, if it were older, would have washed out."

Jenny nodded. "And the person who came here has the key. The door opens outward and there are fresh scrapes in the dirt. What should we do?"

"We need to put a stakeout on this place, and I know just the man for the job."

Detective Gary Linden shivered in the cold. His long underwear and quilted parka did not keep the cold out. He checked his watch. It was three a.m.

*This proves that the Lieutenant hates me. What a miserable assignment! And just who am I waiting for?*

There was a slight rustle behind him. He turned quickly, with his hand on the butt of his revolver. A man came out of the darkness. Gary relaxed. It was Daniel King. He had his finger to his lips. He was carrying a thermos and a packet.

"Jenny sent me," he whispered. "She knew this would be a thankless job, so she sent you something to warm you up."

Gary took the coffee gratefully.

"I'm happy to watch with you if you need some help."

Gary nodded. "Sure, he whispered, but if push comes to shove, stay back. Don't want any civilians getting hurt."

"Sure, whatever you say."

The two men waited, hidden in the brush beside the trail. They had been there for about an hour. Gary checked his watch again. Four a.m. Suddenly, Daniel put his hand on Gary's shoulder.

"Ssshhhh! Someone coming."

Down the trail about fifty feet, they could see the dim light of a flashlight. Whoever was carrying it moved purposefully down the trail until they came to the brush that hid the door. They could see the figure glance around and then stoop down under the brush and push through. They heard a click as the figure unlocked the door, and then heard a creak as the door swung outward. Gary pulled out his revolver and a small flashlight. He and Daniel crept forward. The door was slightly open, and the figure had slipped inside. A flickering dim light, a lantern of some sort, and then they heard whoever was inside come back to the door.

Quickly, Gary jerked the door open and shone the flashlight on the startled face.

Gerhard Müller!

"Freeze," shouted Gary.

Müller did not hesitate, but instantly swung around and knocked the lamp over. At the same time, Müller's hand swept the flashlight from Gary's hand, plunging the cave into darkness. Strong arms went around Gary's neck, cutting off his wind. He struggled vainly to get loose. He could feel himself losing consciousness. Suddenly there was a sound like a ripe watermelon hitting a wall and the grip on his neck released. There was a thud as the man fell to the floor. A flashlight came on and Gary saw Daniel standing over the prostrate body of Gerhard Müller.

Gary rubbed his neck, trying to get his breath back.

Daniel grinned. "I guess he didn't know I was here."

"But I thought you guys were pacifists... You know, non-violent."

"Yeah, well, you won't tell anyone, will you?"

Gary shook his head and chuckled. "Never, I promise. Now I'm going to get some help up here."

---

FLASHING LIGHTS AND POLICEMEN FILLED THE PARKING LOT AT the entrance to the park. Daniel stood beside Gary as a trio of uniformed policemen brought Gerhard Müller toward them. He stared straight ahead. Elbert stepped forward. He took hold of Müller's arm and held it up. A small piece was torn out of the camouflage coat under Müller's wrist. Elbert pulled a plastic bag out of his pocket. Inside was the piece of cloth found in Granny's hand. Elbert placed the piece in the torn spot on the sleeve. It fit perfectly and the camouflage pattern matched. Müller got a very surprised look on his face.

"Didn't know that Granny marked her killer, did you?" He nodded at the officers. "Gerhard Müller, I am arresting you on suspicion of the murder of Jemimah Lengacher. You have the right to remain silent…"

As they took Müller away, Elbert turned to Daniel. "There is something Jenny needs to see. It's in the cave. I want you to meet me here in the morning around 8:00. I think it may tell us what happened back in 1967. All we have to do is figure out why it happened."

THE NEXT MORNING JENNY, BOBBY, DANIEL, AND ELBERT WENT to the hideout. The forensics team had cordoned off the area with police tape and there were two men in uniform keeping watch. Elbert took a key out of his pocket. "We got this from Müller last night." He unlocked the door and swung it open. The heavy wood creaked on rusted hinges. They ducked down and went inside. Elbert turned on a powerful battery lamp and set it on a rock shelf.

Daniel looked at the door framing. "There must have been a small opening here, and they enlarged it, squared it and then framed it in. Easy to do. And this would be a great place to disappear. Way out on the edge of the park in the roughest area."

Jenny looked around. "What did you want to show us, Elbert?"

"This."

He walked over to something covered by a tarp. Before

he uncovered it, he turned to Jenny. "I'm warning you, this is pretty gruesome."

"Go ahead," said Jenny.

Elbert pulled the tarp away. Underneath was a rough wooden chair. Tied to the chair with some strands of rope were human remains. The body had partially mummified. A few bits of stringy, shoulder-length hair remained on the skull. The face was partially gone, blown away. "Looks like someone shot him in the face with a shotgun."

Jenny turned away. "Just as I thought."

Elbert looked at Jenny. "What do you mean?"

"Most murders are committed for one of three reasons, Elbert. Money, love, or power. Here you have three young people spending a lot of time together. Remember what Granny told us? Steven loved Lizzie like a sister, but Aldon was crazy about her. The murdered person in this chair is the terrible thing that happened to Steven and Lizzie. I have my own theories, but I think we need to put Steven and Gerhard together. And we need to run some missing persons reports for July 1967 in the Wooster area and find out who this is. How is the disinterment going?"

"They are digging up the bodies today. And we checked the DNA on the coat piece found in Granny's hand. It's Müller's all right."

Jenny shook her head. "Once you disinter the bodies, you need to check the DNA with the DNA on the coat. If what I'm thinking is true, we don't have a serial killer on our hands. We have a true psychopath."

---

BY THE END OF THE WEEK, THE REPORTS THAT JENNY WAS waiting for had all come in. They arranged for a meeting at the jail for the next Monday. Elbert requested Steven Lambright be brought back from the facility where he was being evaluated. And so, on that Monday, Jenny, Bobby and Elbert sat in a conference room together at the Wooster jail. Two armed guards stood quietly in the corners of the room. At two o'clock the door opened and Gerhard Müller came in, accompanied by more guards. His wrists were shackled, his face impassive.

"I want to have my lawyer present."

"We will contact him and forward your request. In the meantime, there is someone we want you to meet." Elbert turned to the guard. "Would you bring in the prisoner, please?"

The door opened and Steven Lambright walked in. Gerhard Müller stood up.

"What's he doing here?"

"Sit down, please." Müller sank down in the chair. "Steven, I want you to meet someone."

Lambright shuffled over to the table. "Steven, this is Gerhard Müller. But I think you know him under a different name."

Steven came close and looked at Müller for a long time. Then his body jerked as if a massive electric shock had just gone through it. The guards held him until he regained his composure. Jenny noticed that now, instead of wandering vacantly, his eyes had focused. Steven bent over and looked at Müller for a long time.

"It's you," he whispered. "But you are dead."

Müller tried to turn away. "I don't know what he's talking about."

Steven grabbed Müller's arm, turned him back, and looked directly into his face. The guards stepped in, but Steven let go and stepped back. "It is you," said Steven quietly. "You killed him. You couldn't stand that Lizzie loved him, so you killed him."

Müller had paled. "What is this nut-job talking about? I've never seen him before."

Jenny opened a folder in front of her. "Yes, you have, Aldon."

Steven's head moved up and down. "Yes, Aldon... Aldon. It's you. You killed him."

Jenny nodded to the guards. "Help Steven sit down."

Steven slid into a chair across from Müller.

Elbert looked at Lambright. "Killed who, Steven?"

"Ricky Patterson. He killed Ricky Patterson. And then he told Lizzie he was going to kill her. But I knocked him out, and we ran, we ran..."

Steven put his head in his hands and wept.

Jenny opened one of the documents. "This is a forensics report from the bodies of Gerald and Eliza Lehman."

Müller's head snapped around. "What? You dug them..." He stopped.

"Yes, Aldon, we dug them up. After the forensics team examined the bodies, they changed the cause of death. Do you know what they died from?"

"I do not know."

"Oh, but I think you do. They died from arsenic poisoning, which we believe was administered to them by their son. A son who then sold the farm to a phony trust created by a family that never existed, and then faked his own death. After some minor plastic surgery and a beard, that son returned to the scene of the crime and took over his own farm. Only now he was not Aldon Lehman, he was Gerhard Müller." She looked directly at Müller. "We matched the DNA from the Lehmans with the DNA taken from your jacket. You are not Gerhard Müller, you are Aldon Lehman. And you killed your parents because they found out you killed Ricky Patterson."

Aldon Lehman's face twisted into a horrible mask. He stood up, but the guard grabbed him. Aldon struggled. "Yes! Yes, I killed them. They were going to turn me in. Why? Because I killed that stinking hippie that stole Lizzie from me. That was none of their business. I had every right. Lizzie was mine, mine. And I'll kill you, too, you meddling fool." He broke away from the guard and lunged at Jenny. But this time, he found himself in the steel grip of Bobby Halverson. His face twisted in pain.

"I'd sit down, if I were you, Mr. Lehman," Bobby whispered.

Lehman sat.

Elbert stood up and signaled the guards. "Aldon Lehman, I am arresting you for the murder of your parents, Gerald and Eliza Lehman. I am also arresting you for the murder of Anna Myerson, Elizabeth Gingerich Ingersoll, and Missy Berringer."

Steven lifted his head. "You killed Lizzie? You killed Lizzie? But you loved her, you swore you loved her."

"The slut was going to run away with Patterson," hissed Aldon. "Nobody does that to me."

"You also said you would kill me, but you didn't."

Müller laughed. "I didn't have to kill you, you poor mindless fool. All I had to do was set you up. Once they found you guilty, someone else would kill you for me."

"But why?"

"Because you helped her deceive me. You knew she was seeing that junkie, and you helped her. You broke our pact, our blood oath. And for that, you deserve to die as much as she did."

Elbert nodded to the guards. "Well, Mr. Lehman, I don't think that part of your plan is going to come true." He pointed to the door. "Take him back to his cell."

The guards led him toward the door. Then he turned. "At least she's dead. I told her I would kill her and I did. And there is nothing you can do about it. Nothing."

He looked back at Lambright and sneered as the guards led him away.

# ALDON

Jenny watched as Aldon Lehman walked out. She turned to Elbert. "Do you think I could talk to him?"

Elbert looked at Jenny hard. "I don't know, Jenny. He's a dangerous man."

"Not if he's in his cell—and I can talk to him from the hall."

"Let me think about it."

"Look, Elbert, this man grew up Amish. He has caused pain and death in the Amish community. If I could get a glimpse of what makes him tick, it would be helpful to my people. If there is something that we didn't do right when he was a child, if the rules were too strict... I don't know. It's just that he's so twisted up. Maybe I could help him, be someone he could identify with."

Elbert looked at Jenny for a long time.

"Please, Elbert."

Elbert sighed. "Okay, Jenny. When do you want to do it? Not today, though. We still have some processing and legal work to take care of. And he has a court appointment tomorrow morning, an arraignment."

"How about Wednesday afternoon?"

Elbert nodded. "I think that will work. I'll call you after I check my schedule."

"Thank you, Elbert. I appreciate it."

"Well, since you dug up the information that turned this case on its head, I guess I can hardly say no, can I?"

ON WEDNESDAY, JENNY WENT TO THE JAIL. ELBERT MET HER AT the front desk and, along with an armed guard, escorted her into the lockup section of the facility. "Lehman is in a holding cell by himself. We cleared the section, so it's just him in there. You can talk to him through the bars in the corridor. I will be at one end of the hall with Hank, and there will be another guard at the other end. When you get to the hallway outside his cell, there is a line of tape on the floor. I want you to promise me you will not step over it."

Jenny nodded. "I promise."

They walked to a heavy metal door where an attendant buzzed them through, then down a short corridor and through another door. The sound of their feet echoed off the walls mournfully, empty, lost.

Eldon stopped after they went through the second door. "He's right up there. I'll wait here, but I'm close by and I can hear everything. And there's a camera monitoring every-thing you say and recording it. Remember to keep back behind the line."

Jenny walked forward until she passed the wall of the holding cell. The cell was closed in on three sides but open to the corridor. Bars closed in the open wall, so the guards watched the prisoners at all times. At the far end of the hall, a guard sat on a stool behind a small desk. Elbert stood at the near end. Jenny took two more steps and looked into the cell. Aldon Lehman was sitting on his bunk. The light was on in the cell and it lit every corner.

"They won't turn it off."

"Excuse me?"

"They won't turn it off. I like the darkness better."

Lehman turned on his bunk and saw who it was. "Oh, it's you. Miss Nosey Parker, the famous Amish detective. What do you want?"

"I came to talk to you, Aldon."

"Why?"

"I was hoping to get some answers."

"About what?"

"About why you did all these terrible things. Maybe get an idea about what happened to you."

Lehman laughed. It was low and sinister. "What happened to me? What happened to me? That's rich. I'll tell you what happened to me. Lizzie Gingerich happened to me, the Amish happened to me, life happened to me."

He suddenly stood to his feet and took two quick steps to the bars. Jenny instinctively jumped back against the wall. Lehman smiled. "Do I frighten you, Miss Marple?"

"Why do you call me that?"

"Isn't that what you want to be? The Amish Miss Marple?"

"No, I just want to be of help. I want to help you if I can."

"Help? You help me? That's hilarious, Mrs. Hershberger. You know nothing about me. How can you help me?"

"If you could just talk about some of the things you've done, maybe it would help you clear your conscience, get right with God."

A terrible look crossed Lehman's face. "God!" he hissed. "What does God have to do with this? He hates me, He's always hated me."

"No, no, Aldon, you're wrong. God loves you."

Lehman moved right up against the bars, pressed against them, staring at Jenny malevolently. He whispered as his mouth trembled. "If God loves me, why did he give me the parents he gave me? Horrible, twisted people. Playing at being holy and then doing what they did."

"What did they do, Aldon?"

"They tortured me. If I didn't get my chores done on time, they put me in the holding tank."

"Holding tank?"

"Yeah, the grain bin out behind the barn. Only they didn't keep grain in it, just me." He grinned. "That's why I like the dark. I got used to it."

"What else, Aldon?"

"If I wanted something special, they would make sure I never got it. They said it made me too self-centered, too 'in the world' they called it."

"What else did they do?"

"My father beat me while my mother watched. For anything I did wrong, or said wrong, he beat me. Every time he hit me, he would say, 'spare the rod and spoil the child.' I hated him, I hated him."

Aldon put his face in his hands and sobbed. Jenny stepped forward a half step to comfort him, but she remembered her promise to Elbert just in time. Aldon Lehman's head snapped up, and he tried to grab Jenny through the bars, but she was too far back. He wasn't crying now; he was grinning. "Almost got you to come closer, didn't I?" He laughed, a horrible, evil laugh. "You want to know why I did it? Why I killed them? I just... kind of generically hated them

—no reason, really. That made it easy. I killed them because I wanted to. I wanted to see what it felt like."

"What?"

"Yes. When I killed Ricky Patterson, it felt good, very good, almost addictive, you see. So, I wondered what it would be like to kill someone else. They just happened to be in my way. They stuck their noses in where they didn't belong. And it felt good. Surprisingly so."

A chill went down Jenny's spine. "Tell me about Ricky Patterson."

Aldon grinned. "Sure. I killed him, and then I marked him with the 3 X 3 so they could see how they betrayed me. He thought he could just give Lizzie drugs and then sleep with her, use her like a cheap whore, and then throw her away. He didn't love her. I was the one who loved her, me, and she deceived me. So, he deserved what I gave him and she deserved to die, too. And Lambright. He said we were friends forever, that he would never betray our secret—the 3 X 3. But he betrayed me. So, I made them watch, watch me kill Patterson. They were so easy to control. I was going to kill them too, but Lambright found some nerve, shoved me, knocked me out. When I woke up, they were gone. They ran away, far away. But I waited. I knew they would come back to Wooster eventually, especially if they thought I was dead. Leave them alone and they will come home. Like Little Bo Peep." He smiled. "So, I killed myself. Then I left them alone, and they finally came home. Aldon died, and Lizzie felt safe, and Lambright didn't even remember me."

"Why didn't you just kill them both?"

"Too easy. Somebody would have traced them back to me, like that old lady. No, I had to plant a big red herring, stay invisible. Didn't want anyone putting Aldon Lehman and Gerhard Müller together. I knew Lambright was messed up. I keep my ear to the ground, you know. I know everything that goes on around here. When I heard he was back in town but was 'non compos mentis', I followed him. Talked with him at a coffee shop. He didn't know me, didn't remember—lucky for him. So, I thought up this great plan. The great diversion. All pointing to Lambright. And the cops bought it. What a bunch of morons."

"You stole his truck, you bought the tape and the rope, then planted the evidence, probably kept some of his cigarettes for the DNA. And you stole his credit card—so you could buy the evidence in his name."

"You got it all figured out, don't you, Miss Marple?"

"And your parents? Did they really do those horrible things to you?"

"Nah," he grinned, "I fooled you, Miss Smart Detective. I fooled many people over the years. My folks, they were just in my way. So easy. He had been following me, you know. He found my hideout. He saw Ricky. He was going to turn me in, but he got sick before he could. My mother, too. So, I just added a little arsenic to their medicine. I couldn't have him doing that, telling everyone my secrets. Sneaky, sneaky, they all sneak around, spying."

"Who?"

"You, you people, the great God-fearing Amish. All so sneaky. Pretending to be holy, pretending to know God. Maybe you do, but I can promise you, you are serving the wrong one, Miss Sneaky, the wrong God. My God does things for me, he gives me pleasure, he helps me do the things I like."

"What do you like?"

Aldon looked down at his fingernails and then looked up and smiled. "I like to kill people."

Jenny felt another chill go over her. Aldon looked up.

"Frightened, Miss Marple? You should be."

"So those girls you killed? The ones besides Lizzie?"

He smiled again. "They were part of the game. I needed the cops to think Lambright was just a brainless, run-of-the-mill serial killer, crazy from the war." Aldon shrugged. "So, those girls… they just happened to be in the wrong place at the wrong time, more's the pity."

"You didn't know them?"

"Well, I didn't say that."

"You knew Anna Myerson?"

"Anna? Oh, the hiker girl. Pretty, but not smart. She used to walk in my woods. I would watch her when she couldn't see me. She'd be out there all by herself, not a care in the world. Thought she was safe. So, I just walked up behind her and killed her. It was easy."

"What about Missy?"

"Missy? What a slut. I met her at that bar. Sometimes I went out there for a drink. Very high-toned, very discreet. I could be anonymous. Look for people. I was looking for number three. Missy found out I had money, so she started coming on to me. She wanted me to take her home with me, told me we could have a good time. She was so greedy, I didn't have to do a thing. She just walked right into the trap. I went to the club early. I saw Missy and said I would pick her up, told her to meet me at the back of the parking lot after her shift. Pretty secluded, nobody saw her get in the van. But I had to tie her up first, before I killed her." He smiled again, an evil smile. "I marked her before I killed her. I wanted her to think about what kind of girl she was, a loose woman. I'm sure she did. But she didn't suffer long, because we didn't get too far down the road." He giggled. It was a strange sound coming from a grown man.

"And you had Steven's truck?"

"Yep. Missy was surprised. She thought I had a fancy car. And Steven? He didn't even know it was gone. I parked close to the street light down the road before I killed her. And that old lady across the street got the plate number. All part of the plan."

"So, you killed two innocent women so people wouldn't think it was a revenge killing?"

"Something like that. It would have worked too, although I was a little disappointed when I heard they ruled Lambright insane. I wanted him to get the shot. I wanted him to go out of this world, never knowing that I was laughing while he died, wondering how he ended up on death row. I promised them I would kill them, and I always keep my promises."

"What about the man in your car?"

"What man?"

"The man you pretended was you, so you could be dead —back in 1968. The man you killed. There had to be a body in the car, so they would think it was you."

Lehman laughed. "Oh, him. Some bum I picked up hitchhiking. Boy, was he surprised when I stabbed him. Stuck him in the driver's seat, ran the car off the road, then poured gas all over. The Bonfire of the Vanities, I called it. Funny, don't you think? Do you know what a bonfire of the vanities is, Miss Marple? It's the burning of objects condemned by religious authorities as occasions of sin. His sin was he was stupid. He burnt to a crisp. Nobody ever checked it out."

"And you killed Granny because you knew she could identify you. We would have never known about you, except for her."

Aldon shook his head. "You know, for an old lady, she surprised me. I thought it would be simple—sneak up behind her and toss her down the well. But she fought me. Strong. She almost got away. But I killed her in the end."

"But not before she ripped a piece off your sleeve."

He stood closer to the bars, his eyes gleaming. "It's your fault, you know. You didn't have to stick your nose into my business. But you did. And then she told you about me. So, she had to die. She knew me. And you know what Miss Marple? If I could get to you, I would kill you, too." He smiled.

That same chill went down Jenny's back like an icy wind. She turned to go, then turned back. "One more question. You say you fooled many people over the years. Are there more out there, Aldon? More that you killed?"

Aldon turned and went back to his bunk. He looked away from Jenny at the wall. "You want me to draw you a map?"

Almost a whisper.

Jenny turned and ran down the hall. Elbert was waiting, and he caught her in his arms.

"Jenny! Jenny! Are you all right? What did you find out?"

Jenny clung to Elbert. "Oh, Elbert. I have never seen such raw, horrible evil."

Elbert patted her gently on the shoulder as he held her. "It's okay, Jenny, it's okay."

22

# WRAPPING THE CASE

The next day, Jenny and Elbert went to see Steven Lambright. They met him in a sunny reception room on the grounds of the care facility in Wooster. When he came in, he seemed a different man. He had cut his hair short, military style, and he walked with an erect, almost soldierly bearing. His mother was with him. She was beaming as she held onto his arm. The two sat down across a small table from Jenny and Elbert.

"I told you, Lieutenant, I told you."

"Yes, Mrs. Lambright, you did, and you must have gotten through, because it was your faith that got me to enlist Jenny's help. How are you doing, Steven?"

"I'm better, Lieutenant, much better. You know, all these years, it was like I was way underwater. I saw the light far above me. I tried with all my might to get to the surface, but just when it seemed like I might break through, the darkness dragged me back down."

Jenny reached across and put her hand on Steven's arm.

"What happened in that meeting with Aldon Lehman, when you saw him after so many years?"

Steven shook his head. "It was like the floodgate opened. I felt like a million volts went through my brain. And then I remembered—everything. All this time, I've blocked it because it was too horrible."

"The doctor who examined you told us that either a miracle or a tremendous shock to your system could break the blocks that kept you from remembering."

Steven patted his mother's arm. "Looks like I got both."

Jenny smiled. "Indeed. Now, can you answer a few questions so we can clear all this up?"

Steven nodded.

"First, how did you and Lizzie meet Aldon Lehman?"

Steven sighed. "I wish we never had."

He looked away for a moment, then collected himself. "I'll never forget that day. Lizzie and I were out in the woods. We were thinking of building a lean-to or something, you know, so we could have a place to hang out if the weather got bad. But we needed someplace hidden."

"Up on the wild side of the park?"

"Yes. We were looking along the outer trail when we ran into this Amish kid. He was older than us. Seemed to be a together guy. Lizzie and I, well... we were messed up. I mean, I had my dad's death on my shoulders, and her father was..." he grimaced. "You know what he was doing. When we met Aldon, he seemed stable, on top of it, you know. Something we didn't have. He asked us what we were doing, and we told him we wanted to find a hideout."

Jenny nodded. "And he showed you the cave."

Steven looked at Jenny. "Yeah, he showed us the cave. He found it when he was exploring the woods. He said no one knew about it. We started meeting there every day. We brought candles and lanterns, food, some blankets. At first it was fun, very exciting. And then Aldon said we needed to make it safer. It needed a door."

"So, you brought some tools and some lumber," said Elbert, "squared out the entrance, and framed it in."

"Right. Aldon brought some lumber from his farm, and we built the door. We made it heavy so nobody could break in while we were gone. Then one day Aldon said to make it even more safe and more secret, we had to swear a blood oath to never reveal it or our friendship. By then, it was clear he was the leader, so we went along. He had a name for us, the 3 X 3. He made us cut our fingers, mix our blood together, and swear by the 3 X 3 that we would never divulge the secret of our place."

"When did Aldon start acting strange? Bossing you around?"

"How did you know that...?"

Jenny frowned. "I've spoken with Aldon. He is a classic megalomaniac, a control freak. Personally, I believe he's totally insane. I just assumed that at some point in your relationship, he started laying down the rules."

"Yes, he did, and it made Lizzie and me nervous. He was like a father figure or something. He told us what to do, and we did it. It was easier than arguing. Then he got strange. He would do weird stuff like go hunting and when he shot something, he would bring it to the cave and mark it with the 3 X 3. Then he would smear the blood on our faces and make us swear again. It got scary. Then he told Lizzie he was in love with her and he made her promise to let him court her after her *Rumspringa*. He was so insistent that she said yes... But she was just playing him along. She didn't love him, I know that for sure."

"How did Lizzie meet Ricky Patterson?"

"It was *Rumspringa*. Lizzie and I were hitching into town, looking around, you know, checking out the real world. Aldon had a lot of responsibilities on his farm and he couldn't hang out with us as often as he wanted. He wasn't around so much, and Lizzie liked that. His jealousy and controlling ways were getting to her. One day, we met Ricky in the park. He was a nice kid, and we hung out a few times. One of the days we were hanging he told us about the Feast of the Flowering Moon, down in Chillicothe. That's a big deal down there. He was driving down and asked us if we wanted to go..."

THE END OF MAY IN OHIO IS A LOVELY TIME. THE TREES ARE completely greened out and flowers are up everywhere. Steven and Lizzie were waiting in the park for Ricky. Early that morning, they had gone to the cave. Lizzie was super excited about their trip. She left all her Amish clothing at the cave and changed into bell-bottom jeans and a short-sleeved stretch top. She pulled her long hair back and looked very *Englisch.* When Steven saw her that way, he ditched his hat. Then they hitched a ride into town. Around noon, Ricky pulled up in his Volkswagen bug. He leaned out the window and smiled at Lizzie. Long-haired, blonde, a good-looking kid.

"Hey, babe, you look great. Got a jacket or anything? We might get back late."

Lizzie lifted her backpack. "In here. I wasn't born last night, you know."

"Funny. Come on, get in. We have a two-hour drive."

Steven and Lizzie climbed into the car. Steven scooted into the back and let Lizzie sit in the passenger seat.

Ricky started right in as he pulled away. "You guys will

really love this. Native-American music and dancing, traders and exhibits. And they have these mountain-men encampments, you know, like pioneer life back in the day, and all kinds of other stuff. Plus, lots of food. And the best part. It's free."

Ricky looked over at Lizzie. "You got any money? You know, for lunch?"

Lizzie nodded. "Some. Steven has a little too."

"Aww, don't worry about it. Ricky is flush this week. Had some good sales."

"Sales?"

"Yeah, didn't you know I'm a local businessman?"

Lizzie was curious.

"Well, I deal in things that if you ever told anybody, I would get in trouble."

Steven piped up from the back seat. "You mean like drugs or something?"

Ricky grinned. "Yeah... but not dangerous drugs. Just good ol' pot."

Lizzie's brow furrowed. "Pot? You mean marijuana?"

"Yep. Pot, you know, Mary Jane, Herb, Grass, Green Goddess, da Kine..."

Ricky looked at Lizzie and then glanced in the rear-view. "You guys want to try some?"

"Well... I don't know..." said Steven.

"Yes!" said Lizzie.

Ricky grinned again. "Okay, when we get home tonight, you can come and stay at my place. We'll bang the bong."

"Okay," said Lizzie. She glanced back at Steven. Steven just shrugged.

The moment passed, and Ricky kept up a steady conversation. Soon they arrived in Chillicothe. The town was decked out—banners and decorations everywhere. They headed into the downtown area. Before they even got out of the car, they heard the drums and the chanting of the Indian tribal musicians. They walked together through the exhibits. Lizzie was alive, pointing things out and expressing her awe at some of the artwork and clothing. Steven had never seen her so animated. Then they went to the Mountain Man Encampment. The actors had a tent set up, and they had all the tools, traps and guns displayed that the mountain men used. Steven was very interested in that part of the show.

Then the day was over and they were on their way home. When they pulled up in front of Ricky's house, Ricky looked back at Steven. "The invitation stands, bro. Come on in."

Steven shook his head. "I... I think I'll take a pass tonight, Ricky. I don't think I'm ready."

"Whatever, Steven." He looked at Lizzie. "What about you, babe?"

Lizzie looked back at Steven and then nodded. "I'm ready."

"Do you need me to drive you home, Steven?"

"Nah, I'll walk. It's only a few miles. See ya." He looked at Lizzie. "Aldon won't like it."

Lizzie tossed her head. "He doesn't own me."

Steven looked away. "Okay, it's your call..."

Steven sighed. "She loved it, the pot. It made her forget. She could just trip out and everything would go away. Her father, Aldon, her crummy life. She slept with Ricky that night and when I saw her the next day, she said she was in love with him. She started going there every time she could get away. She got high whenever she could. She begged me to help her keep it from Aldon. He was getting suspicious. I told him she was working in town as a live-in babysitter for a family. Then in July I met her at the park. She told me she was leaving, going out to San Francisco with Ricky—to the summer of love. She said as soon as he got some money together, they were going to leave."

"How did Aldon find out?"

"Lizzie was stupid. Ricky knew we had a hideout in the park, Lizzie told him. He wanted to see it. I warned her to be careful, but she didn't listen. She brought him out there…"


IT WAS A HOT SUMMER DAY, THE FOURTH OF JULY. LIZZIE AND Ricky were stoned. They had been wandering through the woods since morning and then Ricky started pestering Lizzie.

"Show me your secret hideout, babe. I want to check it out."

"No, Ricky, Aldon might be there. He's crazy."

"Why do you hang out with a nut-job like Lehman?" asked Ricky. "What's so great about him?"

"He helped us, Ricky. Steven and I were messed up when we met him. He got us to be more focused, look at things differently. But he's gotten very possessive of me. If he finds you at the hideout, he might do something."

"Oh, nuts, Lizzie. I'm a big boy. I can take care of myself."

Ricky reached into his pocket and pulled out a fat joint. "Know what this is?"

Lizzie smiled. "Pot, wonderful pot."

"More than pot, Lizzie, it's Panama Red. The very best pot in the world. I got it from my connection in Columbus. This will take you to paradise."

Lizzie reached for it.

Ricky danced away. "Nope. Not until you show me the hideout."

Lizzie crowded close, trying to grab the marijuana, but Ricky held her away.

"C'mon, Ricky. That's mean. Give it to me."

"Nope, not until you show me the cave."

Lizzie gave up. "Okay, but don't forget, I warned you. If Aldon shows up, there will be big trouble."

They headed for the Outer Trail. Soon they came to the cutoff and Lizzie ducked under the brush and up to the cave entrance. Ricky followed.

"Wow, this is really cool." He tried to open the door, but it was locked.

"Close your eyes."

"What?"

"Close your eyes. I have to get the key and I can't show you where we hide it."

"You're kidding."

"Close your eyes or you can take me home... and I don't give a hoot for your ol' Panama pot."

Ricky closed his eyes. Lizzie reached up behind a rock beside the door and grabbed the extra key. Just then there was a rustling, and Steven came through the brush from the trail. Lizzie put her hand to her mouth. "Oh my gosh, Steven, you scared the peewadden out of me. I thought it was Aldon."

Steven looked scared. "What's he doing here? Aldon will kill us. We broke our blood oath."

"Oh, come on, show me the hideout. I'm not scared of this Aldon character."

"You should be."

They all turned. Aldon Lehman stood behind them. He had his shotgun and a brace of rabbits hanging at his waist. "Who's this?"

"I'm her boyfriend."

Aldon's face paled. "Her what?"

"Well, actually we are a little more intimate than that, aren't we, babe."

Lizzie's face was white. "Ricky, shut up. You don't know..."

Aldon moved closer. "No, Lizzie, you shut up. I want to hear what this greaser has to say. What do you mean, a little more intimate?"

"We're lovers, pal. And we love each other. She's coming with me to San Francisco. She doesn't want to marry you."

"Ricky, don't," Lizzie was begging.

Aldon tossed Steven his key. "Open the door, Steven. Let's go inside."

Steven hesitated.

"OPEN THE DOOR!"

Steven unlocked the door and swung it open. Aldon's shotgun had come down off his shoulder and was now pointing at the three of them. "Inside." He motioned with the end of the gun.

"Wait a minute, buddy, I'm not going anywhere," hissed Ricky.

"I've got a heavy load shot in these shells. If I pull this trigger, and I will, the pellets in this gun will spread out in this cramped space and tear you all to bits. Now get inside."

The three of them backed into the cave. Aldon motioned to Ricky. "Sit down in that chair."

Ricky looked at Aldon's eyes and then sat down. "Steven, grab that rope and tie him to the chair." Steven hesitated again. "TIE HIM IN THE CHAIR!"

Steven quickly bound Ricky's hands behind him.

"Aldon, don't do this," begged Lizzie. "I love him, and I'm sorry. Please, Aldon, please."

"You broke your oath. You swore a blood oath. And now you all have to die. That's the penalty for covenant breakers."

Ricky struggled with the ropes. "Look, pal, I have friends. You can't shoot me. Actually, you won't shoot me, because you're a punk. You haven't got the nerve."

"Ricky! Don't..."

Aldon's eyes looked almost black. "Don't have the nerve? Don't have the nerve? Boy, are you wrong." Aldon laughed. The gun barrel came level with Ricky's face. There was a roar and a flash of light. Lizzie screamed. "RICCCKKKYYY!!!"...

Steven put his head down on the table and sobbed. His mother comforted him. Then the sobs diminished, and he looked up.

"What happened then, Steven?"

"He turned the gun toward Lizzie. He screamed he was going to kill her next. That's when I jumped on him and shoved him. He stumbled backwards and slammed his head into the rock wall. It knocked him cold. I grabbed the gun and hit him again. Then I grabbed Lizzie and shoved her out the door. We ran down the trail. Ricky's car was in the parking lot and the keys were in it. I knew how to drive it, so I pushed Lizzie in and drove her to her house. I told her to get her stuff and meet me at the schoolhouse. I went home and packed my stuff. When Aldon woke up, I knew he would come after us. I told my mom I was leaving and took off. Lizzie was waiting. Ricky had given her some money. We drove to some of her relatives in Indiana and I left her. Then, I went and joined the army. I figured that would be the safest place. The next thing I know, I'm in Vietnam, taking a fifty-caliber slug in the side of the head."

Jenny looked at Bobby. Bobby shook his head. "That's quite a story, Steven."

"I'm just sorry he found Lizzie after all these years. I don't know why she came back. She should have stayed away. She was a good girl, and a good friend."

Jenny sighed. "I'm sorry, too. Sorry for the other girls, and for Aldon's parents and who ever else ran into Aldon Lehman. But at least now we know the truth and the truth can give us some peace."

## THE END...

$\mathcal{E}$lbert and Gary sat on the couch across from Bobby and Jenny. Daniel and Rachel had pulled up chairs. A brisk fire crackled in the fireplace. Outside, an early snowfall covered the ground. Elbert pulled out a notepad and a pencil and handed them to Gary.

"Take some notes, son. You are about to learn a lot." He turned to Jenny.

"So, we know Lehman murdered his parents and Ricky Patterson and Elizabeth Ingersoll and the two other girls, but I don't quite understand what the 3 X 3 thing was all about. Wasn't that dangerous, foolish on his part, as in too revealing?"

Jenny took a sip from her cup of *Kaffee* and smiled. "Well, look at the entire picture, who Aldon Lehman really is. The entire scheme was a ruse to make the police think that there was a serial killer loose and that Liz Ingersoll was just a random killing. Lehman killed three women to hide the fact that only one of them was the target."

Elbert shook his head. "That is really sick. But why did he use 3 X 3?"

Jenny shook her head. "Aldon Lehman is the supreme megalomaniac. He believed no one would ever catch him. In his sick, twisted way, he believed that there was something almost magic about 3 X 3. Once his plan came to fruition, Lizzie would be dead and Steven in prison or executed. He used 3 X 3 as the symbol he was in complete control of the process. No one else knew about 3 X 3 except Granny and maybe Aldon's father, but his father was dead and Aldon didn't know that Lizzie had given away the secret to the old woman. Then, when she told us about the three of them being in a secret club and showed us the 3 X 3, she signed her own death warrant, poor old soul."

Bobby spoke up. "Yes, when Aldon, AKA Gerhard, heard we talked to Granny, he knew he had to silence her. But Granny got back at him from beyond the grave. She fought him and tore the piece off his coat, which led us straight to him."

Rachel spoke up. "But if Aldon wanted revenge, why didn't he just kill Steven, too?"

"Aldon might have if Steven hadn't fit into his plan. Remember, Aldon told me he had his ear to the ground, he knew what was going on. When Steven came home, Lehman heard he was a mental cripple, so he did a test. He followed Steven, went up to him at a coffee shop, and engaged him in conversation. Steven didn't remember him. So, Aldon got Steven to do some handyman work for him and stole his credit card. Once Lehman realized he was safe from Lambright identifying him, he concocted the 3 X 3 scheme to get back at both of them, Steven and Lizzie. He knew Lizzie was back in town. Then, when he was ready to put the plan in motion, he stole the van."

Rachel asked another question. "If Lizzie was so afraid of Aldon, why did she come home?"

"She thought she was safe. She had heard that Aldon died shortly after he murdered Ricky, so that wasn't what was keeping her. What kept her was her father. When he died two years ago, Lizzie finally felt free to come home. Steven came home around the same time, and Aldon, who had just been waiting for them all these years, laid his plans."

"That's why he faked his own death, way back in 1968?"

"Yes, he had the patience of Job. He was willing to wait thirty years to carry out his revenge. He somehow knew that someday Lizzie and Steven would come home. He also needed to disappear and yet stay local. So, he sold himself his own farm."

Jenny smiled at Gary. "Do you remember what Granny told us? When Steven and Lizzie were in *Rumspringa*, Aldon was having to work a lot on his parent's farm. So, Lizzie and Steven were spending time down in Wooster, hanging out with Ricky Patterson without Aldon. Ricky Patterson was a low-level drug dealer in Wooster. We checked the records. He disappeared right about the same time Steven and Lizzie ran away. And the dental records from the corpse in the cave confirmed his identity. From what Steven told us, Lizzie met Patterson and fell in love. Lehman had talked Lizzie into letting him court her after her *Rumspringa*. What he didn't know was that she was not coming back to the church. She was running away with Patterson."

"So, Lehman found out and killed Patterson?"

"Yes, he killed him horribly in front of Steven and Lizzie. Aldon Lehman is a sick, controlling bully. When he met up with Steven and Lizzie out in the woods, he took control of the situation. Both Lizzie and Steven had deep-seated insecurities and Lehman was just the father-figure they both desperately needed."

Bobby chimed in. "What happened at the meeting when Steven recognized Lehman? I thought he would never come out of that fog."

"Remember when the doctor told us that the only thing that would probably bring Steven back to normalcy was a miracle or a powerful shock to his system? Well, as Steven said, we saw both."

"Why didn't seeing him earlier shock him back?"

Jenny shrugged. "Gerhard Müller looked completely different than Aldon Lehman. And Steven was very much out of touch. We were slowly pushing him back to reality and when he saw Lehman at the police station he was able to connect things together. At least, that's my humble opinion."

Bobby smiled. "Like I said, timing is everything in God's Kingdom."

Gary asked another question. "What made you suspect Lehman?"

"Lehman said he knew literally nothing about the Amish, but I heard him use two distinctly Amish sayings. First, when I asked him if he had ever seen any hiding places out in the park, he said, 'No, but then a great deal of what we see depends on what we are looking for.' Then, when I asked him if we could slow the pace so we could look a little closer at the surroundings, he became exasperated and said, 'I won't borrow trouble from tomorrow.' Both are Amish proverbs. He had to be around the Amish when he was young for those sayings to be ingrained in him."

"So, he didn't even think about it when he talked," said Rachel.

"That's right. And the story about when Aldon sold

Gerhard the farm seemed very suspicious to me. Nobody ever saw Müller until months after Aldon supposedly died. And he did the sale anonymously, through a fake trust and by out-of-state attorneys. And one more thing. I checked with Aldon Lehman's bank. A week before he supposedly died, Aldon Lehman withdrew the four hundred thousand he got from the Müller trust from his bank. No one ever found the money."

Daniel scratched his head. "So, Lehman kills his parents because they are going to turn him in, sells the farm to himself, fakes his own death, steals his own money and puts it in his Gerhard Müller bank account. Then he shows up back here months later as Gerhard Müller. Who's buried in Lehman's grave then?"

Elbert shook his head. "I'm afraid that's something we will never know unless Lehman gives us a name. But I don't think even he knows, just some bum he picked up, is what he told Jenny." Bobby asked a question. "Do you think he'll be able to plead insanity?"

Elbert shook his head. "I don't know, Bobby. He's doesn't act insane, like Steven did, so I think when the jury gets ahold of him, he will probably get the maximum penalty. But it remains to be seen." He turned to Jenny. "I guess you were right in getting me to let you talk to him. He certainly spilled the beans."

Jenny sighed. "I got him to open up and confess, but only because we already had the goods on him for Granny's death. He said something very dark when I spoke to him. He pretended that his parents were very cruel to him, that they beat him. Then he pretended to weep. I almost went to comfort him, but just in time I remembered Eldon told me to stay behind the line of tape on the floor. If I hadn't, Aldon would have reached through the bars, grabbed me, and killed me before Elbert could get there. When he failed, he taunted me. He said something very unsettling—I fooled you, Miss Smart Detective. Just like I fooled a lot of people over the years.'"

Elbert frowned. "So, you think there are more victims out there, people that we don't know about?"

"Yes, Elbert, I do. The way people get away with murder is by hiding the crime so well the authorities never find the victim. Or making it seem like whatever happened to a victim just happened during the normal course of life—like slipping someone an overdose of digitalis and everyone just assuming the victim died of a heart attack. That's where Aldon slipped up... well, one of the places. If Doctor Mansfield hadn't had his suspicions, and he had them only because he knew the Lehmans to be very healthy and strong, the Lehmans would have remained buried and we wouldn't be able to prove any of this."

"So that's why you went to see the doctor—to see if he had enough concern about their deaths to sign the disinterment request?"

"Yes. When Aldon Lehman, or Gerhard Müller as we knew him, gave away his connection to the Amish by his language slip, my natural suspicions kicked in. A man that nobody ever met buys a very prosperous farm from a young man who dies mysteriously a few months later. None of it added up. So, I just asked the right questions."

Elbert looked over at Gary. "I hope you wrote all of this down."

"All of it."

"Good. Can you make me a copy?"

Gary Linden looked at Jenny and Bobby. "Whew! Lieutenant Wainwright said I could learn a lot from you and, boy, was he spot on. My head is still spinning. I just hope I learned enough to be more thorough in future investigations, you know, depend on my 'coply' instincts more."

Jenny smiled. "We can only hope." Everyone laughed. "Now, Gary, how about some Amish cake with ice cream?"

Gary smiled and nodded his head vigorously. "Yes, ma'am. For sure."

ALDON LEHMAN SAT ON THE BUNK IN HIS CELL AT THE Wooster City Police Station. In a few days, the state would transfer him to a correctional facility to await trial. His thoughts were dark, bitter.

*She doesn't have the faintest idea who she messed with. I waited thirty years to kill Liz and I can wait to kill Jenny Hershberger. They'll find me guilty, without a doubt, but then I will appeal. Sometimes the appeals process takes years. I can wait. I have the patience of Job. Breaking out of jail is the least of my worries. No, I just need to think it through and carry out the plan when it is time. Jenny Hershberger has not seen the last of 3 X 3...*

Aldon Lehman smiled and lay back on his bunk.

# ABOUT THE AUTHOR

*Patrick E. Craig* is an award-winning author with twenty-two published books. He has won six Chanticleer International Book Awards, a Selah Award and a Word Guild Book Award. His work includes three Amish mysteries six Amish novels, three World War II historical novels and a short story sequel, two anthologies of Amish stories, a standalone novel and a memoir, two western novels, and two YA paranormal books. He lives in Idaho with his wife Judy.

# MORE BOOKS BY PATRICK E.CRAIG

The Quilt That Knew

The Boy In Blue Denim

A Quilt For Jenna

The Road Home

Jenny's Choice

The Amish Heiress

The Amish Princess

The Mennonite Queen

The Journals of Jenny Hershberger

The Amish Menorah and Other Stories

A Christmas Collection

The Gettysburg Letter

Far On The Ringing Plains

The Scepter And The Isle

Men Who Strove With Gods

Beyond The Red Hills

The Drive

Say Goodbye To The River

The Mystery of Ghost Dancer Ranch

The Lost Coast

Contact Patrick at pec@patrickecraig.com

Website: https://www.patrickecraig.com

Find These Books at Patrick's Amazon Page :

https://tinyurl.com/y3nwsmgs

dig into Jonathan's past, Jenny gets serious in her own search for her long-lost parents. And as they travel The Road Home together, Jenny finds the truly surprising answer to her deepest questions, while Jonathan discovers his need for a home, a family, and a relationship with God.

### Book 3—*Jenny's Choice*

Jonathan and Jenny Hershberger are happily settled in Paradise, Pennsylvania on the farm Jenny inherited from her grandfather. But when Jonathan disappears in a terrible boating accident, Jenny and her young daughter, Rachel, return home to Apple Creek, Ohio to live with her adoptive parents, Reuben and Jerusha Springer.

As Jenny works through her grief and despair, she discovers she has a gift for writing. A handsome young publisher discovers her work and, after the publication of her first book, Jenny is on the verge of worldly success and possible romance.

Then a conflict arises with the elders of her church, and Jenny must ask herself if she's willing to go outside her faith to pursue her dreams. At the same time, the budding romance is at odds with Jenny's hope that Jonathan might someday be found alive. Jenny must choose and Jenny's Choice leads her to the surprising and heart-warming conclusion of the Apple Creek Dreams series.

### Book 1—*The Amish Heiress*

Rachel Hershberger's life in Paradise, Pennsylvania is far from happy. Her papa struggles with a terrible event from the past, and his emotional instability has created an irreparable breach between them. Rachel's one desire is to leave the Amish way of life and Paradise forever. Then her prayers are answered. Rachel discovers that the strange, key-shaped birthmark above her heart identifies her as the heiress to a vast fortune left by her *Englischer* grandfather, Robert St. Clair. If Rachel will marry a suitable descendent of the St. Clair family, she will inherit an enormous sum of money. But Rachel does not know that behind the scenes is her long-dead grandfather's sister-in-law, Augusta St. Clair, a vicious woman who will do anything to keep the fortune in her own hands. As the deceptions and intrigues of the St. Clair family bind her in their web, Rachel realizes that she has made a terrible mistake. But has her change of heart come too late?

### Book 2—*The Amish Princess*

Opahtuhwe, the White Deer, is the beautiful daughter of Wingenund, the powerful chief of the Delaware tribe, and a true princess. Everything in her life changes when the renegade known as Scar brings three Amish prisoners to the Delaware camp. Jonathan and Joshua Hershberger are twin brothers that Scar has determined to adopt and teach the Indian way. The third prisoner is Jonas Hershberger, their father, who has been made a slave because he would not defend his family. White Deer is drawn to Jonathan but his hatred of the Indians makes him push her away. Joshua's gentle heart and steadfast refusal to abandon the Amish faith lead White Deer to a life-changing decision, and rejection by her people. In the end, White Deer must choose between the ways of her people and her new-found faith. And complicating it all is her love for the man who can only hate her.

*Book 3—The Mennonite Queen*

**CHANTICLEER INTERNATIONAL BOOK AWARDS SEMI-FINALIST - THE CHAUCER HISTORICAL DIVISION:** This is the third book in The Paradise Chronicles series. Isabella, Princess of Poland, is raised to a life of great wealth and leisure in the Polish Royal Court, destined to marry a king. But fate or divine providence intervenes when she meets Johan Hirschberg, a young Anabaptist who works in her father's stable. This chance meeting leads the young couple into a forbidden love. Together they flee Poland and embark on a dangerous journey that brings them, after great peril, to the small parish of a troubled priest named Menno Simons. Catholic Bishop, Franz von Waldek, paid by King Sigismund, Isabella's father to find the princess at all costs, pursues them across Europe. Isabella does not know it, but if von Waldek captures her, she will have to make a choice that will change the course of European history forever.

# THE ISLANDS SERIES WITH MURRAY PURA

*Book 1—Far On The Ringing Plains*

**CHANTICLEER INTERNATIONAL BOOK AWARDS FIRST PLACE WINNER — HEMINGWAY 20TH CENTURY WARTIME FICTION.**

Far On The Ringing Plains INSPIRED BY TRUE EVENTS In the spirit of The Thin Red Line, Hacksaw Ridge, Flags of our Fathers and Pearl Harbor. Realistic. Gritty. Gutsy. Without taking it too far, Craig and Pura take it far enough to bring war home to your heart, mind, and soul. The rough edge of combat is here. And the rough edge of language, human passion, and our flawed humanity. If you can handle the ruggedness and honesty of Saving Private Ryan, 1917 or Dunkirk, you can handle the power and authenticity of ISLANDS: Far on the Ringing Plains. For the beauty and the honor is here too. Just like the Bible, in all its roughness and realism and truthfulness about life, reaching out for God is ever-present in ISLANDS. So are hope and faith and self-sacrifice. Prayer. Christ. Courage. An indomitable spirit. And the best of human nature, triumphing over the worst. Bud Parmalee, Johnny Strange, Billy Martens—three men that had each other's backs and the backs of every Marine in their company and platoon. All three were raised never to fight. All three saw no other choice but to enlist and try to make a difference. All three would never be the same again. Never. And neither would their world. This is their story.

*Book 2—The Scepter and The Isle*

**CHANTICLEER INTERNATIONAL BOOK AWARDS FINALIST — HEMINGWAY 20TH CENTURY WARTIME FICTION**

It did not end with Guadalcanal. It did not end with one island. There were more islands... an island with snow-capped peaks, friendly people, blue seas, where Bud found love with his Tongan princess. Where Billy breathed the clean air of mountains where no danger lurked. Where Johnny found a way to drain the hate that drove him mad. They found life again after the death-filled frenzy of Guadalcanal But the God of war was not done with them. More islands sent their siren call from beyond distant horizons and they were cast upon dark shores. Islands with coconut palms, dense green jungle and death. Islands that took more life than they ever gave back. Islands where women killed like men, islands filled with the most brutal soldiers the Japanese Empire could offer. Tarawa. Saipan. Islands that had to be endured. Islands they had to survive. There was no other way to bring the war to an end. There was no other way to get home again.

*Book 3—Men Who Stove With Gods*

**CHANTICLEER INTERNATIONAL BOOK AWARDS FINALIST — HEMINGWAY 20TH CENTURY WARTIME FICTION** Since 1941 the Marines have fought the Japanese. They met them first on Guadalcanal, a maelstrom of death and fury. Tarawa, Saipan, Okinawa—their friends died beside them, their youth disappeared in a baptism of fire, but they kept on. Johnny, Bud, and Billy went ashore on bloodstained Okinawa hungry for the end of the war. But they knew when the battle ended, they would face their Armageddon on the sacred beaches of Japan.

phone and computer and TV, and settle in for a good night's read. Craig's book is a blessing.

— **MURRAY PURA,** AUTHOR OF *THE WINGS OF MORNING* AND *THE FACE OF HEAVEN*

A good storyteller takes a fine story and places it in a setting peppered with enough accurate details to satisfy a native son. Then he peoples it with characters so real we keep thinking we see them walking down the street. A great storyteller takes all that and binds it together with, say, a carefully constructed Rose of Sharon quilt and the wallop of a storm of the century that actually happened. *A Quilt For Jenna* proves Patrick Craig to be a great storyteller.

— **KAY MARSHALL STROM,** AUTHOR OF THE *GRACE IN AFRICA* AND *BLESSINGS IN INDIA* TRILOGIES.